Somewhere Within Us

Somewhere Within Us

Ulla Bolinder

Translated from the Swedish by

Eric Swanson

in collaboration with the author

Originally published in Sweden as *Någonstans inom oss*

by Anamma, Gothenburg, 1999.

Everyone is a world by Gunnar Ekelöf
translated by L. Nathan & J. Larson. Princeton, 1982, p. 42

Cover photos: Pixabay

Publisher: BoD – Books on Demand, Stockholm, Sverige

Print: BoD – Books on Demand, Norderstedt, Tyskland

ISBN: 978-91-7699-780-2

Love is letting someone

be what he or she is.

Arthur Janov

Lasse and I have repapered our bedroom walls. Already when we moved in, the wall paper was worn, and now we have lived in the apartment for almost ten years, so it needed to be done. Especially where the beds stand the wall had become tarnished.

It doesn't seem as if we have lived together for so long as ten years. The time has passed, but nothing has happened. If we had had children it would perhaps have felt different, but we cannot have any children. I have been sad about it and don't think of it anymore. What Lasse feels I don't really know. He doesn't say very much. I suppose that he has accepted it. In any case, there is nothing that can be done about it.

Kicki, my best friend, doesn't have any children, either, but that's because she hasn't met the right man yet. All relationships she has had so far, have ended. But she thinks it's about time now, that the love of her life and the father of her unborn children turns up.

Every Saturday we visit Lasse's parents and every Sunday we go to mine. It's convenient not having to prepare dinner on weekends, but I don't think it's especially fun to be together with them. Well, with Lasse's parents it's okay, because there we talk, and Lasse and his dad and I usually play cards, but with my parents it is as dead as it has always been. There isn't anything to say, and everything feels just painful. I hate listening to papa trying to discuss politics with Lasse and seeing how mamma put it on. I almost feel sick and just want to leave. Why do you have to be on visiting terms with people you don't have the least in common with? I don't want that.

But we can't continue having contact with Lasse's parents at the same time as we break off relations with mine. And how can I explain to them that we don't want to visit them anymore? What should I give for a reason? That I think they are so stupid and limited that I can't stand being in the same room as them? I can't say that. And you must do your duty.

Henrik, a young guy who substitutes at the medical bath where I work, has an alcohol problem. He has come to work under the influence, and now my female work-mates have had a serious talk with him and discussed what they should do to try to help him. I haven't noticed that he has felt bad, but he admitted to them that he drinks too much.

Well, I see! And what do they think they should be able do about that?

When I was sixteen years old I drank a lot. Kicki and I hung out with the *raggare* on Svartbäcksgatan at that time, and there it was easy to get hold of spirits. In the beginning I took it as a pleasure to be drunk and didn't understand that you may drink because you are unhappy, and not just because it's fun. Alcohol can be an anesthetic for mental pain, but I didn't realize that in the beginning. Some who have drunk for a long time find perhaps other ways to ease their pain and stop drinking – they become sober alcoholics – but to be free you must get to the bottom of your problems, and you can't force anyone to do that.

No one has asked me what I think ought to be done to help Henrik. I think my work-mates believe that I'm too well-behaved and inexperienced to know anything about alcohol abuse. But I know that they can't help him. They can possibly get him to stay sober at work, but they can't get him to stop drinking. He must want to do that himself first, and I don't think he has come to that point yet. He has a buddy who works at the internal transport, and one day when that guy came to us with a patient, I heard them decide to meet in the evening and go out and have a grog.

When I started to be together with Lasse seriously, I stopped drinking. That was also when I was sixteen. Since then I have only been drunk at parties sometimes. Nowadays it almost never happens.

Lasse doesn't drink very often either, and Kicki is a total abstainer. Her papa is an alcoholic, so she has always been an opponent of booze, but as a teenager she drank sometimes anyway, just to join me.

We smoked and drank. Now I'm the only one who does it, because she has stopped smoking as well. I know that smoking is damaging to your health, and I know that it hinders mental pain from entering consciousness, and I hate to feel tied to ensure that I always have cigarettes at hand, but I continue all the same. If Lasse didn't smoke, it would perhaps be easier for me to stop. But I must manage even so, because otherwise I'll never get to know the truth, and without the truth you'll never be free.

Kicki lives alone now, and we usually meet each other at her home. But a few years ago, when she was together with a guy called Åke, we almost lost contact, because I didn't like him, and I couldn't understand what she saw in him. He was like a mussel from whom it was impossible to get a sensible word out. Lasse perhaps doesn't talk very much either, but you can have a normal conversation with him anyway.

Though it's only with Kicki I can express all I want. Every time we meet, we share what has happened to us, and then we discuss and analyze it. We are like two serial stories that never end.

I don't think you can be like that with a man, because men are not very interested in themselves and not as emotionally penetrating as women. Not in my experience anyway. Though Lasse is the only man I have been together with in that way. And for the most part, it depends on how good emotional contact you have, if you can talk with each other or not.

One day when Henrik's buddy Johan sat in with us and waited for Henrik to be finished to go home, he started to solve a crossword in an old weekly news paper. When I went by, he called me to come and help him with a word that he couldn't figure out. "Hetaera" it was above, and in the middle of the word there was an 'o' and a 'k' already written.

"It will probably be 'hooker'", I said.

"Aha", he said and looked at me and smiled.

I don't like when people say or do things that I don't understand the underlying meaning of.

One of the women at work is driving me crazy. Her name is Astrid. If I am busy cleaning a bathtub, for instance, she can come in and place herself beside me and stare at me without saying anything. And if I ask her what she wants, she just comes up with some trifle that doesn't explain what it really is. It makes me very annoyed, and I just want to push her away, but I become as paralyzed and don't know what to do to put a stop to it.

Why does she act like that? What does she want? Why can't she just let me be? I have tried to act indifferent and uninterested, and I have tried to avoid her and to only give short answers when she asks me something, but nothing has helped. It seems that she doesn't notice or care that I'm dismissive.

And if I did what I really feel, and told her to go to hell, everyone would think I were nuts, because nobody can possibly be angry with Astrid who is so kind and sweet!

But what should I do to get rid of her? What should I do to make her understand that I don't want anything to do with her?

I have been together with Lasse for eleven years, and as long as we have lived together, I have never been unfaithful to him. Once, a rather long time ago, I was interested in a guy at work, but it was only from a distance and nothing I was serious about.

I don't think that Lasse has been unfaithful to me, either. This summer we have been married for five years. Directly after our wedding at city hall, we departed on our honeymoon to Dalarna. We had rented a cabin there, which we stayed in for a week.

Kicki isn't married, but she has been engaged two times and lived with three different guys. She has not been unfaithful, either. Well, she has, but only when she has wanted a relationship to end.

If I happened to meet a guy that I felt physically attracted to, I would never go to bed with him if I were not in love with him also and knew that I would rather live with him than with Lasse. But from a distance, and in secret, you can be interested in others without doing any harm.

I happened to hear an old song from the '60s on the radio – "Anyone Who Had a Heart" with Cilla Black – and that made me start thinking about what has become of my dreams and hopes from that time. "Anyone who had a heart would take me in his arms and love me true." It hasn't gone quite the way I thought, I have to say!

But I'm not unsatisfied with my life, even though there isn't very much happening on the love front just now. Eva-Lena, my best friend, is comfortably off, married and settled as she is, but I think I have a hard time settling down. And when things have been calm and restful once in a while, I haven't been satisfied with it.

I remember, for example, how it was when I was engaged to a boy called Bosse, and I started going out with my sister to dance. She and her husband were going to get divorced, and I was feeling a bit fed up in my own relationship and thought that nothing was happening with Bosse and me, so I started to go out.

And one evening I met another guy. I can't say that I fell in love with him, but when he proposed that we should meet again, I went along with it. We met at first when we were out dancing, and then sometimes in pri-

vate. And one evening – and I don't know why I did it, because I didn't actually want to – it happened that we lay with each other in his car.

Afterwards I thought: Now it's over! Not because it had been a failure, but because it was as a confirmation that there wasn't anything between us, and that everything was some sort of action against Bosse on my part. At the same time, I was flattered by the attention and the shown interest, because I felt that Bosse had cooled off concerning that.

And all at once, I told him everything. Then he collapsed and thought that we should break our engagement and move apart. Yes, and I thought that it was just as well that we did. I took it very easily, I remember, while Bosse looked more and more miserable for each day that passed. Finally, he sat one evening in the leather easy chair in the living room and tore and pulled on his undershirt, so a hole was worn in it, and he looked so miserable that I softened and asked him what it was. Then it came out that he was sorry, and that he not at all wanted it to end. I had been in the firm conviction that it was just as well that we separated, but when he became that sad I melted, and so we reconciled and continued.

I have been to mamma and helped her with her hair. She wanted it washed and set, and I helped her with that. Afterwards, I sat with her a while and talked. She didn't feel especially alert and needed to take oxygen several times, and I think it's so sad that she must be sick!

It started when she got a cold, and then it developed into pleurisy. And when she came to the hospital, it turned out that she also had emboli in both her heart and lungs. I felt guilty about it, because it was I who had given her hormone injections, which had been prescribed for her by a gynecologist for her menopausal difficulties. It's surely because of those shots she has gotten emboli! I though. Because there is a calculated risk that emboli can develop because of hormone preparations. And she didn't get well and had to start with oxygen.

A few years earlier, papa had got early retirement pension. Actually, he should have been fired, because he had begun to tipple at work. But before that happened, an accident occurred. He lost his foothold when he stood on a metal ladder and caught one leg between the stepping pins and broke it so the bones stood out in two places.

For that reason, he was home all day, and finally mamma couldn't cope with him, because he couldn't cope with her being sick. When he had drunk only a few beers, he was annoyed and couldn't tolerate anything. He scolded her and was impatient, and she tried not to cough to avoid bothering him.

And that was what finally drove her to get a divorce from him. Finally, but too late, because she has never had any joy in her freedom. She has got it more peaceful, but she can never do what she wants because she is sick.

Eva-Lena called and asked how I felt when I fell in love with Bosse and how I could be certain that I loved him. I don't really know why she was interested in that, all of a sudden, but I answered as well as I could.

I met him in Funbo, when I were there with a friend and danced. I was sitting alone at a table, when a guy called Gurkan walked up to me and invited me to dance. He had been drinking and was drunk, and I didn't want to dance with him or speak with him, but he sat down beside me and started talking. He tried to hold me and kiss me also, and I felt more and more bothered and didn't know how to get rid of him. Then another guy suddenly came across the dance floor and up to me and asked me to dance.

And that was Bosse. He came like an angel to the rescue, and I was so relieved that I said yes immediately. Then we danced several dances during the evening, and when it was time to leave, Solan and I got a lift with him and his mate in their car. They drove us home, and in the car Bosse asked if he could see me again. It wasn't love at first sight from my side – and not from his either – but I thought he seemed nice and said yes. How long it took afterwards before I realized that I was in love with him, I don't remember.

Speaking of being drunk, it seems that Eva-Lena has begun to drink again, after a break for more than ten years. She claims that it's related to a young guy who she has met at work. But she seems so confused, *and I don't quite understand the reason for it. I can understand if she worries about that it can become difficult in her relationship with Lasse, if he should find out that she is interested in another, but that doesn't seem to be the reason. And she probably doesn't expect to be forced to tell him about it. But in that case, whatever she feels for that guy can't be especially serious.*

Before Christmas, Eva-Lena and I intended to apply for an evening class in English in the spring and study a little during our free time. We meant to start at the gymnasium level. Actually, we have that knowledge already, but it doesn't do any harm to refresh one's memory, we said. We have normalskolekompetens, *which is what the exam from the girls' school was called. It's more than* realen *but less than* studenten. *But our intentions came to nothing.*

At that time, when we still went to school, Eva-Lena wanted to be a journalist, I remember, and I was thinking about becoming a psychologist or a nurse.

But I never studied beyond the girls' school. I was together with Bosse then and wanted to move away from home as soon as possible, so I began to work directly after school. I got employed as an assistant nurse at Kungsgärdet's hospital. Eva-Lena worked first at Salabacke-

tvätten and later at a restaurant, before she came to the Academic Hospital, where she works now. I sometimes think that I should continue to educate myself within health care and get an exam, but so far nothing has come of it.

Elsa, one of our patients, is very trying. I know that she hasn't had an easy time in her life, with a man who drank and a son who is a drug addict, but I react negatively to her behaviour all the same.

It's worst in the mornings, before she has been washed and dressed. Then I don't know how many times she can ring. And when I come to her, she says: "Help me sister, help me, I think I'll faint!" But there isn't anything physically wrong with her in that way, and everyone knows that she is only shamming.

The thing that makes it tough for me, I believe, is that her helplessness reminds me of my mamma. I have difficulty tolerating her aura, which says that she wants to be taken care of. It gives me the creeps when I'm near her, and I feel that I want to distance myself from her, but because I know that my reaction is related to mamma, I never express it.

Why has it always been so difficult for me to assert myself and express what I feel?

When I was little, there was always so much nagging from papa's side at the dinner table, I remember. "Sit properly on the chair!" and "Don't butter on that side!" and so on. There was so much that was to be exactly his way. But I never dared to protest or be angry.

I couldn't be angry with mamma either, because she took such offense at it. To her I was most often surly instead. But I have gotten angry with her later. Once I was close to hit her. I don't remember now what it was about, but I stood in front of her about like papa and said: "God, how I would like to smack you!"

That I haven't been able to object, must depend on that I have felt hindered – partly because of papa's anger, and partly because of mamma's despair – and I don't think I'm really free from it yet.

I have been interested in a guy at work. His name was Johan. He worked at the internal transport and was a friend of Henrik, who substituted with us previously.

The first time I saw Johan I thought: I'm not afraid of you. I don't know why that thought appeared in my mind, because I couldn't know how he was when I had never met him before. It was as if a voice inside me said it to him in my thoughts.

But it took a while before I realized what I felt for him. In the beginning, I believed that I felt unsure and confused when I talked to him just because I didn't understand him. And I didn't want to fall in love with a much younger guy. I didn't want to fall in love at all. I tried to avoid admitting that I had. But I was waiting for him every day and hoped that he would come in with patients, so I would get a chance to see him. I was disappointed if he didn't come and upset when he did. Finally, I had to admit the truth to myself.

Now he is no longer at work. If I had known that he would disappear, I would perhaps have told him that I was interested in him, but I thought that we had plenty of time, and I was afraid that he would become afraid and deny that what I felt was mutual, if I went straight to the point.

Now I don't know what to do. I hoped that I would stop thinking about him when I didn't meet him any-more, but it hasn't turned out that way. I felt so close to him, even though nothing was said or done… But he probably thought that I was too old, because once he called a girl my age a hag. I don't know how old he was. Twenty, perhaps.

I have found out Johan's telephone number. I don't know what the purpose of it is, because I dare not call him. Just thinking of doing it, makes me upset. He pro-bably wouldn't remember me, and it would be so dif-ficult to explain to him who I am. What would I say? "Hello, this is Eva-Lena, do you remember me?" No, I can't say that. And what else would I say? That I love him and want to see him?

I could perhaps send him a letter, to give him time to think about it and get used to it. But I don't know. The best thing is probably to let it be and try to forget him.

Once when I came out to the parking lot at work, I caught sight of Johan, who was scrapping some ice away from the wind shield on his car. One front door was open, and just as I went by, he took out a sheep-skin and shook it, at the same time as he looked at me.

I don't know what happened then. It felt like an invisible power tried to draw me to him. I had to force myself to continue walking, because my legs became totally stiff, and I almost couldn't move my feet.

I had thought that I wanted to come along with him to his home, but I didn't want to scare him, and if you do things that aren't guided by reason, you have no control over the consequences.

But now I have written a letter to him. I didn't sign it, because it expresses his feelings as well as mine, and I believe that he knows nevertheless that it is from me. "I love you", I wrote. Then I took the letter with me when Lasse and went shopping and asked him to stop at a mailbox. I didn't think of it then, but now I find it strange that he didn't ask me what I was going to post, because I usually never send any letters.

But he didn't say anything. He stopped the car, and I climbed out and went up to the postbox. My legs felt totally stiff, and when I dropped the letter in the box, it was as if two strong forces collided in the air above. It was like a discharge, like in a thunderstorm, but invisible and without sound. It was heaven and hell that met, I believe. But I wasn't afraid, because I knew that I was in the right.

Heaven is God and truth, and hell is the devil and lie. If you deny yourself and what you feel, you leave an opening for the devil to come in. Then he takes place in your soul and forces you to do things that you don't want to do. To be free you must disclose all lies that you have believed in and admit that you're worth real love. That's why the devil tried to scare me so that I wouldn't send the letter to Johan.

I love you.

I have started to drink again. It's strange that Lasse hasn't said anything about it, because I haven't drunk this much since it was over between us eleven years ago. He hasn't asked why I do it, and he doesn't seem surprised. He just accepts it without a word.

Sometimes he drinks a little himself, but never so much that it shows. In the beginning, I offered it to him, but he doesn't like vodka and wine, so now he buys his own booze. Though he doesn't drink as often as I, and not as much. He doesn't like to lose control, he says. He thinks it's beneath his dignity to be loaded and not know what he says and does.

But it's not beneath *my* dignity. When I am drunk, I am able to know what Johan is feeling. I can identify with him, so that I become him. Sometimes it's he, and not me, who lives here. Emotionally it's he, and rationally it's me. And I go along with it, because I don't want to be separated from him.

Once Lasse began to talk about girls he was together with before he met me. Them he has never told me about. But he told Johan, when they sat here and drank together.

I want to meet you.

I have sent Johan a postcard that depicts the castle and Svandammen. I went up to the kiosk by the cafeteria and bought it. I am the castle that he can live in if he wants to, and his long-necked swan is welcome to swim in my pond.

I know that he perhaps gets angry when he receives cryptic messages, but if you don't understand with your intellect, you can react more easily emotionally, and I know that his feelings can comprehend my pictures.

When I dropped the card in the mailbox, an old man nearby began to whistle a melody that mamma used to sing when I was little. "When spring comes to the mountains, may I come to you then?"

It was a sign, I think. Subconsciously, other people perceive my need for Johan and try to give me information about him. If I listen emotionally, I can get to know it.

The best thing, of course, would be to meet him in reality. I have written to him and told him that I want to do that. But I don't know how it can be done. When he wants to get a girl, he usually goes to Baldakinen and dances. If I dared, I could go there also and perhaps meet him. I wonder how it would feel to dance with him – if I could dance, that is. But he would never ask me.

The easiest would be if we met in a car. There you are secluded, and you can do what you feel without having to worry about what other people would like and think about it.

But how can we meet in a car if he never comes and asks if I would like to ride with him?

Do you want to meet me?

The last time we were at Lasse's parents, and Lasse and his dad talked about something that I didn't listen to very carefully, I heard Lasse say: "You don't help an alcoholic by being a half alcoholic yourself."

I became upset and felt stung. At the same time, I thought that it isn't applicable to Johan and me. He is not an alcoholic, and I don't think that I help him by drinking. It's what I get to *learn* about him when I drink that can be of help, and when I know enough, I won't need to keep on with it anymore.

A guy who just had come back from a desert expedition reported:

"On the third day the whiskey was gone, and on the fifth day the beer was gone."

"But didn't you have any water?"

"Water? Who the hell is thinking of washing himself in that situation?

Once when Johan sat in the caretaker's office, and I happened to pass by, he called me.

"Eva-Lena!" I heard. "Come here!"

In front of him on the desk he had an open weekly.

"Do you know why the Norwegians have stopped using ice cubes in their grogs?" he said.

"No?"

"Because the guy who knew the recipe for ice has died."

I laughed then, but actually I didn't want to, because it felt as if he were trying to joke away that he wasn't happy. I think that you should admit and experience the pain instead of denying it.

I looked at his neck and shoulders and took a ruler that lay on the desk and drew it over his hair. He sat motionless and let me do it without objecting.

Afterwards I thought: Why did I do like that? I didn't understand it, but now I think I know the reason. There was no physical limit between us, and that's why I felt that I had the right to do whatever I wanted with him.

I want to marry and have children with you.

Eva-Lena and I have been to Solveig, an old classmate from the girls' school. We went there to congratulate her on her birthday. We usually gather with the one of us who is having a birthday and eat a little and talk. It's a nice tradition, I think. This summer it's ten years since we finished school, and since then we have maintained contact.

When it was over between Bosse and me, Solan and I went out and danced sometimes and traveled on vacation together, but we don't do that anymore. The last time we have done something together, was probably when I was together with a guy called Åke, when we traveled to Rhodes.

He didn't want me to go then, I remember. I think that he probably felt that I had begun to get tired of him and was afraid that I would meet someone else. He wasn't certain about me, anyway. Once he had read in my little pocket almanac, where I had written about Peter, a guy whom I had met at Baldis, that the physical had felt so natural and relieving with him. And considering how difficult Åke had had it in that area in the beginning, he took offense at it. But I was angry with him then. What the hell did he mean by reading in my book? It wasn't exactly a diary, but anyway.

And it was true that I had begun to get tired of him. I thought that he was so childish. The day before Solan and I would depart, he got sick with high fever, and he probably believed that that would make me stay home. But I said quite cold-hearted, that he should call the doctor if he didn't get better, and then I went away. I knew that his reaction had something to do with his mother, because once he had told me that he had tried to keep her remaining by becoming sick. But that didn't get me to stay home, luckily. I wasn't that dumb, at least.

And when I got home, I told him that I had been turned on by a guy on Rhodes. I hadn't gone to bed with him, but Åke became very upset about it, because he probably thought that I shouldn't have been involved with anyone at all, I guess. But for my part, I thought I had been strong who had managed to say no to that guy.

Now Eva-Lena has begun to realize that she has never loved Lasse. I have suspected that since the day they began being together, but she has always claimed the opposite.

I remember once, when they hadn't gone steady for so long, that she told me that she almost never felt any desire to lay him. "But in that case, you can't be in love with him!" I said, which was the first thing that popped up in my head. But oh yes, she absolutely was, and she could never think of breaking up with him! And I hadn't exactly expected her to be glad and thank me and say: "Yes, you're absolutely right about this, how dumb I am, that's of course the reason why I don't get excited, now I must go immediately and break up with him!"

I hadn't expected that, but it felt as if she closed herself completely to what I said, and I wasn't ready for that. I had doubted already from the beginning that he was the right one for her, but then it was as if I saw it even more clearly, at the same time as I realized that she didn't want to see it.

But now she had played poker with him and got a flush in clubs, and that she took as proof of that they aren't suited for each other. "And we can't solve crosswords together," she said. "Oh, is that also necessary?" I said, kind of jokingly. Yes, because she had done that with Johan – the guy at work – and then she had realized that many things also have a deeper meaning, that she hasn't been aware of before. "It must feel as if I am two," she said, "and with Lasse it has never felt like that."

I have been to mamma again. We came, among other things, to talk about how it is – and how it has been – between her and me, and I said that it feels tough for me *when I notice that she wants me to be like a mother to her. "Do you really want me to take care of you?" I said. "Yes!" she replied and looked completely delighted in her eyes.*

I think it's so terrible that she actually wants that, because I have believed that she still has wished that she could take responsibility for herself, though she hasn't been able to do it. I became so disappointed when I realized how little she is.

But she has always shown it. It's just I who hasn't wanted to see it. Once, when I was six or seven years old, she took my teddy bear, that I had gotten from grandma, and stood in front of me and held it so I saw that she needed it much more than I. When I think about it now, and see her standing there with my teddy bear, I want to say: "It's my teddy bear, mamma!" I should have said that when I was little, but I never did.

Lasse won't get to touch me anymore. He doesn't care about my feelings anyway. He could lay anyone, because he only masturbates when he has sex. He doesn't lay me out of love, and to go along with it in that case, isn't right.

I didn't know what love was, before I met Johan. If I should be able to love and help him as much as he needs, I must first love myself, and to let myself be used is not loving myself. You must begin with yourself and learn to be true and honest with *yourself* to be able to be that way with others. As long as you don't say no to what is wrong and stop doing it, you can't say yes to, and be filled with, what is right. There is no room for it then.

Right or wrong it got to be.

On Saturday, I was with a friend and drank wine. I don't exactly know how much it was, but when I was about to go home I felt a bit tipsy. I walked on Svart-bäcksgatan and thought of all the times I went drunk there as a teenager, when Kicki and I were *raggarbrudar*. Later, when it was over between Lasse and me, I drank every weekend for four months. Then he came back, and I stopped.

Now I have started again. Kicki thinks that I have been able to stay away from drinking thanks to Lasse. During all these years, it has been Lasse instead of the bottle for me, she believes. But that I have started drinking again has nothing to do with him. I can do without both him and the spirits.

What a hell of a street to be winding, said the drunk, struggled to get home. (Saying)

I have seen Johan. He came in his car and passed the bus stop where I sat. When I met his gaze through the windshield, my legs became totally stiff. His face was also stiff.

He looked like the last time I met him, when he and another guy came walking in the culvert at work. It seemed like he didn't think of greeting me, but when they came nearer, his gaze was drawn to mine almost as against his will.

"So long," I said and looked into his eyes.

"Bye-bye," he said.

His face was totally expressionless, as if he tried to hide what he felt, or as if he thought it was unpleasant to greet me. I don't know. But if he had been completely indifferent, he wouldn't have looked that way.

This time we didn't greet. I don't know why. But I don't think it was a coincidence that he drove past where I sat. I believe that he is drawn to places where I am without being aware of it himself.

What a hell of attraction, said Wahlström, ran to the pub.

(Saying)

I don't know what to do, to make Lasse understand that I don't want to lay him, and that he doesn't have the right to compel me by force. Why doesn't he care about what I say? It must be my own fault that I can't get him to understand that I'm serious. In the evenings, when we have gone to bed, I just lie there and worry about that he will start trying again.

I don't want to sleep in the same room as he anymore. I want my own room, which can be locked, so that I may be left alone.

Johan is the only one I want to lay. Sometimes I fantasize that he comes to work and pulls me into an empty room and strips my clothes off and presses me down on the floor and does it. Once I imagined that he and two other guys waited for me outside the entrance, and when I came out, I was raped first by one of them and then by the other, while Johan stood next to us and watched. He was the one who had told them to do it, because he wasn't able to lay me himself, and I knew that it was more painful for him to see it, than it was for me to be subjected to it.

It hurts to think of it. If he could realize why he is afraid of me, the pain would disappear, and he would be free to do whatever he wants.

Here dances Mr. Cucumber, both waltz and mazurka!

This thing that I feel against my right groin, must be a penis. I want to lean forward and suck on it, but that's impossible, because you can't reach it. How long have I had it? I don't mind having it, but I still hope that

Johan will be able to take responsibility for it himself soon, because as long as it's I who feel it, we can't have sexual intercourse, and that's something I would really like to have.

The tap in the hole, said the cooper. (Saying)

Sometimes when I identify with Johan, it feels like a big, dangerous animal begins to move inside me. Don't be afraid, I think, it's just repressed feelings that are brought to life.

But it doesn't help. My thoughts are not able to keep it under control. They can't stop it from extending and taking over.

I must let him have all the space he needs. I can't deny him, as perhaps his parents did when he was little. I must acknowledge him and help him to be free by opening myself and making his unaware emotions aware.

I will never deny or abandon him.

> Somewhere within us we are always together,
>
> somewhere within us our love can never fly
>
> Somewhere
>
>   o somewhere
>
> all the trains have left, and all clocks stopped:
>
> somewhere within us we are always here and now,

we are always you not far from confusion and
confounding,
we are suddenly wonderment of wonder and transformation,
breaking sea waves, rose fire and snow.
(Out of Arioso by Erik Lindegren)

Hasse, a guy at work that I have tried to help a little with his alcohol problem, turned up at my home one evening. I sat at the kitchen table and wrote, when I suddenly saw him come walking outside on the exterior corridor, and I realized immediately that he had been drinking, so I only opened the airing window and asked what he wanted. I don't know if I told him outright that I didn't want to let him in because he was drunk, or if I just said that I didn't want to talk with him, but something dismissive I said.

Then he started to cry. If I wasn't willing to listen to him, he would throw himself over the railing, he said – and disappeared. I thought I saw him falling down on the inside, but I had to go out and check if he had hurt himself, because I had heard a thud. So, I rushed out, and there he lay like a pile on the floor.

After that, I let him come in. He sat in the kitchen and began to talk, and what it was about I never understood, but suddenly he grabbed my arm and held it in a grip as hard as iron. He looked completely wild in his face, and it passed through my mind that he might beat me to death, because he seemed totally absent and preoccupied with his emotions.

But I didn't show how afraid I was. Instead I began to talk quietly, like to a child, so that he would let go of me.

And finally, he did. Suddenly he passed out and fell off the chair and down onto the floor. Then I called for Lasse. I explained the situation to him and asked him to come over and help me to get rid of Hasse.

But before Lasse got here, Hasse came round and set off. I saw him collapse down on the lawn. And then I still felt rather calm, but as soon as Lasse entered the door, the shock hit me. I could hardly speak, and he scarcely heard what I said, because I just stood there and shook. Yes, and he held me, and finally I calmed down, though I still felt upset and was near tears.

I don't know why I reacted so strongly to Hasse's behaviour. Now afterwards, I think that it must have been because of his restrained anger, which awakened in me some old denied fear that I haven't been aware of before. But I can't say for sure where it comes from.

The last time I talked with Eva-Lena, she said that she can feel as if she has a penis, and that she is sexually excited almost all the time. Sometimes, when she is at work, she must go into a toilet and masturbate to get some relief. It can happen to her at any time, and she can't resist it. "It's probably like this with young guys when their sex drive is strongest," she said. She is completely occupied with feelings and thoughts about sex and doesn't know how to deal with it. You can possibly guess that her infatuation with Johan has awakened a sleeping dog, and that's why she feels so strongly right now, but I don't really know.

It reminds me of how it was when I was turned on by a guy called Peter. I met him at Baldakinen, and right from the beginning I felt an irresistible physical attraction to him. We danced a lot during the evening, and then we went to his home, and there we ended up in bed. I wasn't in love with him at all; it was just a purely physical attraction that made me do it.

I was together with a guy called Leif then, and the physical intimacy with him wasn't good at all. I had almost begun to believe that it was me who had the problem and thought: Is it my doings that make it this strange? But when I had been together with Peter, I understood that it wasn't because of me.

Then I was going to break up with Leif. I knew that it would be difficult, and to strengthen myself I went to Peter's home one more time. He didn't have a telephone, so I couldn't ring beforehand, and when I got there, he wasn't home. But his mate was there, and I sat down and waited. He could have come home with a girl or whatever, but I didn't think of that. And then he came, and I didn't need to explain why I was there, because he immediately understood it, and we went to bed again.

The next evening, I met Leif and broke up with him. It made him cry, but I managed to do it thanks to Peter. Before I had felt so weak, as if I wasn't sure that I could go through with it. But now I said to him that our relationship didn't feel good to me, and that I didn't think we matched. But whether I expressed that I thought that our sex life was bad, I don't remember. I don't think I said it straight out. But he knew about it anyway, because I had tried to talk with him about it several times before, during the half year we had been together.

After my first escapade, which I made myself guilty of when I was together with Bosse, things were fixed between us again, and we had it rather good for a while, except for my occasional small outbursts. If we sometimes fell out, he took it very calmly, and I could get irritated about that, because I flared up more easily. He wasn't very much for talking about how things were, either, and that made me feel that he didn't care enough about us.

And one day he came home and said that he had decided to move. He didn't think that things were functioning for us any longer and would move and live with a friend, he said. By then we had been together for six years and had lived together for almost five. We tried to talk, and he didn't usually get angry, but then he was so upset that he took the transistor radio and threw it into the wall, so it crashed and fell into pieces.

At the same time, I had been stricken with salpingitis and had been given medical leave for an entire month. I was in the country with mamma and papa then, and the next time Bosse came out, I wanted to talk, of course, and find out why. At first, we were upset, but then I thought: If only he can be alone for a while, of course things will be good again, since he is in love with me. I took it easy, which made him a little surprised, but it didn't change anything, and he maintained that he would move.

And eventually, I understood that we wouldn't just be apart from each other for a while, and then start all over again, but that the intention was that this should be the end. I appealed to him and begged that he should come out to the country again, and I said that if there was any possibility at all, that he would some time think that we could start over again, he should come out on Saturday.

And on Saturday I went out to the road at the time I reckoned he should turn up and waited. But he didn't come, and when I realized what that meant, I lay down on the ground and just wanted to die. It felt so dreadful and I was so miserable. And I don't know if mamma and papa felt sorry for me, or if I convinced them to drive to town, but we drove home anyway, and then I sat down and started to call around after Bosse.

I found him with a friend in the bushes outside of Almunge. There he was, and he had drunk a little and couldn't drive. No? Could he come on Sunday then? Yes, he promised that he would come the next day, so that we could talk.

And then he came on Sunday, and I thought that he probably would soften, but he didn't. Though for me the worst was already over then, and we agreed that we would part as friends.

Eva-Lena seems completely occupied by the guy she became interested in at work. She says that she can identify with him and take in his feelings. Sometimes she can be like paralyzed or feel so sad that she lies on the floor and twists herself in pain, and she believes that it is his feelings she perceives and expresses on these occasions. She claims that he lives within her. Every time they met at her work – he isn't there any longer – he got in more and more without her perceiving it, and now he fills a vacuum in her that she didn't know she had, until he came in and filled it, she says. She believes that she stays in emotional contact with him all the time.

But how does that work? Does that contact happen telepathically then, or what…? I really don't know what to think about it. I rather suspect that he has disordered her emotionally, because he reminded her of something from her childhood that she has denied and repressed – for that's what we believe in, after reading The Primal Scream. *That this should be about a common infatuation or love, doesn't seem especially likely to me.*

In Suzanne Brøgger's famous book Deliver Us From Love, *which I have borrowed from the library, it says among other things: "If a man can have an erection and ejaculate within a woman who has not shown any desire, then you must draw the conclusion that he is totally alienated – not only from the woman, but from himself and all reality."*

It makes me think of certain things that Eva-Lena has told me about Lasse – that he tries to force himself on her against her will – and if that is true – and of course it is – you can't deny that the description fits him. But can it really be that bad?

I believe that the purpose is that Johan and I shall be the first loving couple on earth. When we have experienced all denial emotions, and have let us be filled with ourselves, we will be able to love unselfishly. It will be a struggle of life and death. But now that I know how threatened the devil feels by love, I'm no longer afraid. I'm aware of the fear, but I don't allow it to control me.

Though sometimes I doubt that I do right by writing to Johan. Don't do it, don't do it! I hear, and then I become uncertain. I don't know to whom the voice that protests belong. Some letters I never send away.

Once when I was on my way to the postbox I decided to try to interpret and follow all the signs that appeared on the way there. First, an old man stopped me and asked for directions, and that made me feel convinced and determined, but then I was almost hit by a boy on a bike, and when he shouted "fucking bitch" at me, I was hesitant and tore the letter apart and threw it away.

There are a lot of things that can get in the way. If I, for instance, take a cigarette before I have posted a letter, it can happen that I become doubtful and don't know if I should post it or not. Therefore, I don't smoke then. And not when I'm writing, when I'm sober, because the smoke suppresses all feelings, so I can't distinguish between right and wrong.

You leave room for the devil when you smoke.

If you faint in the day of adversity, your strength is small.

(Proverbs 24:10)

I think that I see Johan everywhere. He drives the bus which I ride, he dances in the entertainment program that I watch on TV, and I see his car at a distance when it turns around a street corner or is parked among a hundred other cars at a parking lot. I'm aware of him all the time, both outside and inside of me.

I don't understand what's happening. There are two worlds, but it's just the over world that is perceptible. I don't believe there are many who can interpret signs from the underworld, though this is the one that is most important. Because, it is from this world everything in the over world is controlled. I have not been aware of the underworld before, but now I know that everything people say and do has a double meaning and must be translated to the underworld's deepest sense, so that you shall be able to know the truth.

…In every world thousands of souls are trapped,

in every world thousands of worlds are hidden

and these blind, these underworlds

are real and living, though incomplete,

as true as I am real.

(Out of "Everyone Is a World" by Gunnar Ekelöf)

One evening when Lasse drew the bedroom curtains, which were not quite dry after washing and ironing, I became angry and said:
"Lay off the curtains! You're making them dirty."
Then I realized that Johan doesn't want me to let Lasse touch my labia. And it's not because of him that they are moist, either.
I don't want to lay Lasse anymore. Johan is the only one I want. Sometimes I fantasize that we sit in the back seat of a big car which slides slowly along the street, and while we cruise I press myself against him and pull down the zipper in his jeans and take out his

penis. I have a skirt on, and I take off my panties and sit astride him and put his penis in me at the same time as I kiss him. He is passive the whole time and thinks that what I do is mentally unpleasant, but he can't stop me and say no, because he is so randy.

Nervous Heart Trouble, typical difficulties at n. are heartbeat, sometimes in the form of a quickened heart activity, but more often in the form of a heartbeat that feels stronger. So called extra systoles are common, the heart seems to "stop" or "do a somersault" etc. With closer investigation the mechanism reveals itself to be such that an extra heartbeat comes very tightly after the previous one, whereupon there is a longer pause. This peculiarity occurs to some people without them having any discomfort; others feel an unpleasant kick in their bodies, have a depressing feeling of the heart staying still or something similar. This symptom can present itself in connection with heart disease, but in most cases, it is not a dangerous phenomenon and presents itself mostly with persons who have a nervous disposition. The symptom often disappears on its own and is often improved with medical treatment.

(Medical Reference Book)

I send postcards and letters to Johan several times a week. I can't resist writing to him. Sometimes he gets cassettes with music. I try to awaken his unaware pain, so that he can take responsibility for it himself. When I write letters I'm not cryptic, and I don't try to make him react only emotionally. In the letters I mostly express myself clearly. But I believe that I make him feel, whatever I do.

The Letter The Box Tops

Stranger Billy Swan

Stand by Me The Searchers

Sweet Nothin's, Brenda Lee

Hurt Timi Yuro

Bridge Over Troubled Water Simon and Garfunkel

SOS ABBA

When a Man Loves a Woman Percy Sledge

Out of Time Chris Farlowe

Silence is Golden The Tremeloes

Sloop John B. The Beach Boys

I Can Help Billy Swan

Heart of Stone The Rolling Stones

Ring, Ring ABBA

Rock 'n' Roll Music The Beatles

Johnny B Goode Chuck Berry

When You Walk in the Room The Searchers

One Nigh Elvis Presley

To Know Him is to Love Him The Teddy Bears

Only the Lonely Roy Orbison

The End of the World The Caretakers

Together P. J. Proby

I felt ill and intoxicated, though the only things I had drunk was coffee and water. Is he drinking now? I thought. Is that why it feels like I'm drunk?

But I don't think that I have to be affected by everything he does. If I call him and show him that I know that the sickness doesn't belong to me, it will perhaps pass away, I thought.

I felt nervous as soon as it had passed through my mind. I became sweaty in my hands and shaky in my legs, and my heart pounded so I could hardly breathe. But at last I called.

"Johan," he answered.

"Are you drinking now?" I said.

Then he hung up without a word. But as soon as I had said it, my feeling of sickness was gone, and I think that proves that it belonged to him.

This need putty, said the painter, lay drunk behind the fence.

(Saying)

I have been to mamma. We sat on the balcony and had just drunk our coffee, when the doorbell rang. I went in and opened the outer door, and I caught sight of papa standing there, with a kitchen lamp in his arms. He stepped into the hall, and I knew that mamma wants him to take off his shoes, so I told him to do that.

Then he became angry and blurted out that it was none of my business, or that I shouldn't give a damn about it, or something like that. He wasn't quite sober, so he flared up immediately. And I shouted at him that he should go to hell, which led to that he stood directly in front of me and said: "Watch out, or I'll smack you!" And I answered: "Yes, do that, because I'm no longer afraid of you!"

When I came home I thought about how I had expressed myself, and then I realized that I have perhaps been afraid of him anyway, though I haven't understood it. Otherwise, I wouldn't have said that I no longer am afraid, I mean.

Yes, it was of course because of that I became so upset when Hasse came home to me and threatened me! It was the fear of papa I felt then! Before, I had repressed it, but then it came out. When I was little I behaved so that he never had a reason to be angry with me, but I saw how he acted towards mamma and Anita, and unknowingly it of course made me afraid of him.

Lasse called and was concerned about Eva-Lena. He wondered if I have noticed her changed behaviour. He said that she drinks several times a week, and often just lies on her bed and stares at the ceiling or sits in an easy chair and listens to music. Sometimes she locks herself in the bathroom and refuses to open, and when he asks what she's doing, she doesn't answer or comes up with some strange explanation that he doesn't understand.

He asked me if I know what's wrong with her. And I do know in some ways, but as long as she isn't ready to tell him about Johan, there isn't much I can say. I said that I think she has wound up in some kind of crisis – the thirty-year crisis, you have heard of! – and the best thing is to let her be for now. I felt that he wasn't satisfied with it, but it was the best I could achieve.

You can wonder how Eva-Lena manages to reconcile her drinking with her conviction that you should not escape from the truth, because according to the primal theory, alcohol abuse is an escape from painful feelings repressed in childhood.

And I believe in that. I believed it very strongly when I met a guy called Sven and wanted to help him with his drinking problem. He should go with me to the country, I thought, and stay there as long as necessary. He wasn't *allowed to bring any spirits with him, and if he didn't drink, feelings would soon well up, and there he was isolated and could scream and give free release of his pain, I thought. Oh, yes! But the most that happened, was that he helped me with my vegetable gardening.*

Later he was at Ulleråker. Once, when he took a pass, we met at Fågelsången and had coffee. It was so sad, I remember, and I was so upset, because then we talked about Lena, his girlfriend. He and I had not been together sexually more than possibly three times, and I didn't want it to be more than that, but I wished that he would choose me anyway, because what he and Lena had together, I thought was wrong. He said it himself, that he had the depth with me and the easygoing with her, and therefore I thought that he should decide on me.

But he couldn't refrain from her, if he and I didn't have a physical relationship also. When he told me that, I was sad. He didn't choose himself then, I thought, and there are several others in my life who haven't done that.

Eva-Lena has been here. On the bus here, she started feeling ill and felt ready to faint because a drunk guy had climbed in. She had begun to feel as bad as he actually did, if he had been able to feel it, she said.

During the evening she talked a lot about Johan and how she believes she is being affected by him. It isn't enough that she claims that she has reexperienced her own birth – and that's quite possible if you have accepted Janov's theories – but now she has felt how it was when he – Johan, that is, not Janov! – was born, and that I think sounds a little too incredible. She had had some sort of primal experience of it in the bathroom one evening, she said.

And once her leg had become stiff and started to shake concurrently with feeling: I don't want to, I don't want to, please mamma, let me be! But it was not her own mamma she was thinking about then, and not herself she was trying to protect, because she had felt more like a boy and thought that all of it actually belonged to Johan.

And I don't know. She always sounds so convincing when she speaks, and sometimes I actually become a bit deranged in my belief about what is possible and not. She referred me to a book called The Dialectics of Love, *in which it says that love is not just an* incorporation *with the one you love, but a* change *of the couple's ego. But I don't think that is especially common.*

Anders, my sister's son, is now thirteen years old. That means that it's eleven years since I lost my virginity. I came to think of it when I visited them to hand over a birthday present to Anders, because then Stig, my former brother-in-law, showed up unexpectedly to congratulate Anders. Yes, Good Heavens! I have thought many times that I should tell Anita what happened between him and me once upon a time, but nothing has come of it yet.

I was almost seventeen, and Stig was twenty-eight. Anita was in the country with Anders and his little sister, who was new-born then, and one evening Stig called and asked if I would like to come over. "Sure," I said, because I had nothing special planned for the evening, and I thought it could be fun to meet him and talk for a while. I took my bike and rode away.

And when I got there, he had just showered and came and opened the door in only his bathrobe. And there was nothing special about that, but then he asked me if I wanted some whiskey – Vat 69, which he had bought – and I accepted. It tasted like hell, but I drank it anyway and became intoxicated.

And eventually, we ended up in the bedroom, on the double bed there. He carried me to it, because I was so under the influence that I was wobbly and had difficulty walking. And in that condition, you don't feel much resistance, you really don't, so I let it happen. I let him take my virginity, as they so prettily put it. I can't say for sure that I would have said no if I had been sober, but I think so, because even though I had had a crush on him for several years, I had never thought that it should go as far as to sex.

But he wasn't that drunk that he didn't know what he was doing. When I reflect on it now, I actually believe that it was planned from his side. Both that he had bought spirits and that he took a shower just before I came, indicates that.

But I don't accuse him of tricking and seducing me. It was I who let it happen. I didn't say no. I was so drunk that I couldn't have done much about it, but I could have said no thanks to drinking. Subconsciously I must have understood what he was out for when he offered me spirits, but that didn't make me refrain.

And if you have said yes once, you can say yes one more time! He called a few days later and asked if I wanted to come over again, and I don't know what I was thinking, but I got my bike and rode away. And when I got there, it was no time until the same thing happened again! But this time it was during the day and I was sober.

After that I decided that it shouldn't happen anymore. Considering Anita and the children, I thought it should never be repeated. But I didn't regret it. In a way it might have been better if it had never happened, mais je ne regrette rien.

Johan has called! He has called, and I have spoken to him. "Thank God that he has begun to talk, said the old woman, when the little boy lay in the cradle and swore." He didn't know who was writing to him, until I sent him my personal code number, so that he could find out, he declared.

I don't remember all we said. It feels much like trying to remember what you have talked about when you have been drunk. But I hadn't drunk anything. *He* had possibly done it, but not me.

"If you really like, we can continue this game," he said. "But shouldn't we try to agree in another way?"

"This is no game," I said.

"No, but I can't have it like this any longer. I can't cope with more of your letters."

Then he asked if Lasse knows that I am writing to him.

"Is he there?" he said.

"Yes."

"Is he making difficulties?"

"No."

"Is he drunk?"

"No."

"Tell him to come here, and I'll give him a blow!"

"Why?"

"You become jealous if you like someone."

I didn't understand what he meant. Who did he think had a reason to be jealous? He himself or Lasse?

Afterwards Lasse asked me who had called.

"It was Johan," I said.

"Johan? And who the hell is that?"

"A guy at work."

I didn't say that he isn't there any longer. I became so upset talking about him, and to admit to Lasse that he exists, that I almost couldn't speak.

"What did he want?"

"Nothing special."

"Why the hell did he call, then?"

"I don't know."

"Sure as hell you do! Don't you think I understand what you're up to!"

"No, I don't."

"With him you want to do it, won't you? For him you're so fucking horny that it drips along your legs!"

"Yes, that's possible," I said, because I had decided not to lie.

"When are you going to move in with him then?"

"I don't know about that. Probably never."

"Never? So, you'll just run over to him and let yourself be fucked by the bastard whenever you're dripping?"

"No."

"No, you're perhaps thinking about doing it *here*?" he said scornfully.

"Yes."

Because we already do, though Lasse doesn't know about it.

In the evening he wanted to lay me. When I objected, he tried to force me to give him a blow job instead, though he knows that I think it's disgusting.

"But with that fucking bastard you wouldn't mind doing it, would you?" he said. "You wouldn't mind giving *him* a blow job! And that's perhaps what you're doing, when you say you're going to town. Then you sit there with your skull in his crotch while he's driving. Then you sit there and enjoy sucking cock!"

He is angry, but I'm glad that he knows about it now, because I don't like to mislead him. And sooner or later I would have been forced to tell him about it anyway.

For he does not know what is to be, for who can tell him how it will be? (Ecclesiastes 8:7)

When I had done the dishes, I lay down on my bed and fell asleep. I dreamed about Johan, that he worked at a hospital, and when I came there, he offered to help me with my bags. I was not sick, but I would be admitted, and he came and met me in his white coat.

After a while I woke up because Lasse was laying on top of me. I didn't manage to react before he had pulled up my skirt and forced my legs apart.

"Now it would be nice to have a bang!" he said.

I didn't want to, and tried to throw him off, but he held fast.

"If you want to do it with the bastard, you also want to do it with me!" he said and pressed my arms down.

When I saw his red, exited face above me, I started to growl and show my teeth like a mad dog. I felt how my facial muscles contracted out of hate and disgust, and when his face came closer, I threatened to bite him.

"You must be completely out of your fucking mind!" he said and let me go.

He thinks that I'm mentally ill. He has said that. He doesn't understand that I just change places once in a while.

The human is like a dead, when she is intoxicated by wine. But she is as mentally ill when she is obsessed with love. (Pythagoras)

I went with Lasse on a picnic. He parked the car at the side of the road, and we went into the woods and sat in the shade on a blanket. I was a little afraid that he would try to take advantage of the situation, but he didn't. We just drank coffee and ate biscuits and buns that we had brought.

After a while it felt as if the air began to tremble of tension. I tried to ignore it and continued to drink my coffee, but it didn't disappear. The air vibrated as from a restrained power, and everything felt threatening and frightening. It's perhaps the end of the world that is approaching, I thought.

A little later, I caught sight of a downy insect that crept up on the blanket, and then I understood that it was a sign from the devil who wanted to show that he was present. When I looked up again, I noticed a guy in yellow bathing-trunks who stood at a stone a bit away. There was no lake nearby and no pathway, so it was strange that he stood there in the middle of the woods almost naked.

"Fucking peeper!" Lasse said, but I knew that it was the devil in a different shape, so I kept quiet to not confirm him even more.

This seems to go straight to hell, said the priest, as the horses bolted against the church wall. (Saying)

You don't have the right to use someone else when you masturbate. Lasse has used me, but if we had had mental contact, he wouldn't have been able to do that. You must have emotional contact when you have sex. What's the meaning of it otherwise? If you don't love each other, you shouldn't sleep together. Sex should be an expression of love and nothing else.

I shouldn't have let him touch me. Because it wasn't me he touched, and there was no feeling for *me* he wanted to express when we had sex. And now he shouldn't be able to lay me at all, I think. He shouldn't be able to get an erection, when the only thing he feels is hate. I don't understand how it's possible.

A guy was carrying on with push-ups in the park. A drunk lurched up and stared wide-eyed at the guy.

"Hey, you," the drunk finally said, "haven't you noticed that the broad has left?"

I have called Johan. Lasse had gone out, and as soon as I was alone, I knew that I would call. My heart pounded, and my hands shook so I almost couldn't dial the number, but I forced myself to do it, because if you let fear prevail, you'll never be free.

I awoke him, I think, because I heard him fumble with the receiver before he said his name.

"I love you," I said and hung up.

I needed to prove that I dare to say it also and not just write it. That's why I called. Afterwards I felt relieved.

I love him, and I want to give him everything he needs. What he needs most of all is himself. How can I give him that?

By acknowledging and bearing those parts of him that he has denied, until he is able to take care of them himself.

For now we see in a mirror dimly, but then face to face. Now I know in part; then I shall understand fully, even as I have been fully understood. (1 Corinthians 13:12)

When Lasse and I were at his parents, I put my head under the water in the water butt and held it there as long as I could, to prove that I'm not afraid of what is hidden and buried beneath the surface. I will find out what it is and receive it.

I can already feel the levels and see the differences. In the underworld nothing can be explained, and nothing can be understood. There are no words, and feelings without words is chaos. I know how it feels when there is a connection between the overworld and the underworld, and I know how it feels when the connection is broken. All messages that stream in, must be interpreted, but it's difficult to get thoughts and feelings to come together.

I must withdraw even more and leave even more room for feeling. I must be totally filled with it, to know the truth. Because I have promised to never deny and abandon him.

There are doubtless many different languages in the world, and none is without meaning; but if I do not know the meaning of the language, I shall be a foreigner to the speaker and the speaker a foreigner to me. (1 Corinthians 14:10-11)

I have seen Johan again. It was on the beach, when Lasse and I were there the other day. At first, I thought I just imagined it, because I usually think I see him everywhere, but it was really him. He had black bathing-trunks on, and he went out on the bridge and dived in.

Lasse felt suddenly so unfamiliar to me. I couldn't

understand why I was sitting there with him. What had I to do with him?

Sometimes it feels almost as if I hate him. Everything he does that he has no right to do… Why should I put up with that? The last time he tried to force himself on me, I spit in his face. Then he threw me aside and screamed that I was insane. When I defend myself, and show him what I feel, he thinks I'm crazy.

But I don't give a shit what he thinks! I don't want to live in the same place as he any longer. I want to live with Johan. I will write to him and ask if I can do that.

May I live with you?

Unknown guy: Hi, why are you standing here?
  I: I don't know.
  He: You don't know?
  I: No.
  He: Are you waiting for someone?
  I: No, not exactly…
  He: Well, the river is beautiful in the evening.
  I: Yes.
  He: Would you like to take a walk with me?
  I: No, I can't.
  He: Why not?
  I: Because I can't walk.
  He: Why not?

I: …

He: What have you done earlier tonight?

I: Been to the movies.

He: And now you are standing here waiting?

I: Yes.

He: Yes, there are a lot of cars driving by here on the street…

I: …

He: May I ask what your name is?

I: I don't know.

He: You don't know?

I: …

He: Do you need help in some way?

I: …

He: You aren't considering… taking a swim, are you?

I: No.

He: Why are you standing here, then?

I: Because I can't move from here.

He: Why not?

I: Because I can't walk.

He: Are you hurt somewhere?

I: No.

He: Why can't you walk, then?

I: …

He: Do you want me to call you a taxi?

I: No, that's not necessary.

He: But you can't just stand here.

I: …

He: Do you live nearby?

I: No.

He: Where do you live, then?

I: I don't know.

He: You don't know your name and you don't know where you live?

I: No.

He: Then I think you need you some help.

I: …

He: Do you want me to help you?

I: …

He: Are you certain that you don't want me to call a car, so that you can come home?

I: Yes.

He: Okay.

Male voice 1: Hello! Why are you lying here? Aren't you feeling well?

I: …

Male voice 2: Is she reacting?

Male voice 1: No. And she doesn't smell of spirits… Hey! Are you sick? Do you need help?

I: …

Male voice 2: Her breathing is normal.

Male voice 1: Yes. Check the pulse to be sure.

Male voice 2: It seems normal.

Male voice 1: And she isn't drunk… What the hell could it be? Hey! Do you hear me? Can you open your eyes?

I: …

Male voice 1: No, she's completely gone. She has probably taken something. We'll check her arms and see if she has any needle marks.

…

Male voice 2: No, nothing here.

Male voice 1: Not here, either. But it must be some damn way to bring her round. Hey! Do you hear what I say? Why do you lie like this? Are you sick?

I: …

Male voice 1: Take away her hair so that you can see her face.

…

Male voice 1: Hey! Do you hear me? Can you answer?

I: …

Male voice 3: What's going on? Is she drunk?

Male voice 2: No, it doesn't seem like that. But it's not possible to bring her round.

Male voice 3: Is she maybe epileptic?

Male voice 2: Yes, that's possible. But don't they usually have a badge or something on themselves?

Male voice 3: Yes, I think so.

Male voice 1: Check her purse to see if she has anything there. There's nothing here, in any case.

Male voice 2: Not here, either.

Male voice 3: It's probably just as well that you call an ambulance. She can't lie like this.

Male voice 1: Yes, you're right. Do you have time to

stay here, while I go and call?

Male voice 2: Yeah, no problem.

Male voice 4: What's up? Has someone died?

Male voice 2: No.

Male voice 4: Is she drunk?

Male voice 2: No, but it's impossible to establish contact with her.

Male voice 4: She's completely gone?

Male voice 2: Yes.

Male voice 4: How long has she lain like this, then?

Male voice 2: I don't know. We... I came recently.

Male voice 4: Well, she's probably under the influence of some shit...

...

Female voice: What has happened? Has she fainted?

Male voice 2: I don't know, actually.

Female voice: But why is she lying here? Is she unconscious?

Male voice 4: She's probably just drunk. Hey, babe, jump up now and don't lie here playing the dying swan!

Female voice: Did she just collapse?

Male voice 2: No, she was lying like this when we came.

Female voice: Shouldn't we try to get her up?

Male voice 2: No, that's probably not advisable.

Female voice: Is she injured?

Male voice 2: Not that you can see.

Female voice: What's wrong with her then?

Male voice 4: It's probably just love trouble. It will pass.

Female voice: Oh, my God, what shall we do? Why does she sound like that? Can't she breathe?

Male voice 4: Take it easy, damn it!

Female voice: But it's probably an epileptic seizure. Shouldn't we put something between her teeth, to prevent her from biting her tongue?

Male voice 2: I don't know.

Female voice: But what should we do? Should we just let her lie like this?

Male voice 2: It's okay. The ambulance will soon be here.

Male voice 4: Hi, it's been a long time! How are you?

Male voice 5: Well, I'm fine. What's this, then?

Male voice 4: The devil only knows… Some junkie chick who has caved in. Have you been to the movies?

Male voice 5: Yes.

Male voice 4: Same with me.

Male voice 5: What has happened?

Male voice 2: I don't know.

Female voice: She's hyperventilating and has convulsions.

Male voice 5: Has someone called an ambulance?

Male voice 2: Yes, it's on its way.

Male voice 5: Is she drunk?

Male voice 2: No, just under the influence of pills, I think.

Male voice 4: Do you still live in Norby?

Male voice 5: Oh, yes.

Female voice: Now the ambulance is coming.

Male voice 4: And you are busy working?

Male voice 5: Yes, the same as usual.

Female voice: Now she's calming down.

Male voice 2: Yes, that's fine. And here they come. Let's hope she gets help at the hospital.

Ambulance guy 1: Hello.

Male voice 2: Hi.

Ambulance guy 1: What's happened here?

Male voice 2: I don't know. She lay like this when we came. We couldn't establish contact with her. And then she got some kind of attack and started…

Female voice: … hyperventilating.

Male voice 2: Exactly.

Ambulance guy 1: Okay. Can you move a little aside then, and let us pass.

Female voice: But what can be wrong with her?

Ambulance guy 2: It's hard to say.

Female voice: She isn't drunk then?

Ambulance guy 1: Could you please give us some space here.

Female voice: Poor her.

Ambulance guy 1: Do you have hold of her?

Ambulance guy 2: Yes.

Ambulance guy 1: Okay. Ready to lift. One, two, three.

Female voice: Oh no, now she's starting again! My God, how scary! Why does she act like that?

Male voice 4: Perhaps she doesn't like to be strapped?

Female voice: Is she in pain somehow, or what is it?

Ambulance guy 2: Take it easy now and try to relax.

Female voice: Is she afraid?

Ambulance guy 2: Just take it easy. There is no danger. We're here to help you.

Male voice 4: Let go instead, and let's see what she does.

Male voice 2: Did she faint?

Female voice: Why are you doing like that? What's the use of it?

Ambulance guy 1: …

Female voice: It's some kind of heart massage, isn't it?

Ambulance guy 2: The pulse is unchanged.

Female voice: Is she unconscious?

Ambulance guy 2: Can you please pick up the shoe there. Thanks.

Ambulance guy 1: Okay, now we're done here. Bye, then.

Female nurse 1: Hello, Eva-Lena.

I: …

Female nurse 1: Has she lain like this the entire time?

Ambulance guy 1: Yes, she has.

Female nurse 1: She hasn't looked up and she hasn't said anything?

Ambulance guy 1: No.

Female nurse 1: Okay, we'll take care of her.

Female nurse 2: Do you hear me, Eva-Lena? Now I'm taking off your jacket, so that the we can examine you.

I: …

Female nurse 2: Yes, here we go… And now I'm going to draw up the sleeve and set on a blood pressure gauge.

I: …

Female nurse 2: Is room two available?

Female nurse 1: Yes, it is.

Female nurse 2: Now it tightens a little around your arm here.

I: …

Female nurse 2: That's it… And now we'll take a blood sample. Do you hear me? You'll soon get a stick in your arm, and meanwhile you must lie completely still, so that nothing happens to the needle. Do you understand what I say?

I: …

Female nurse 2: Could you hold her arm while I do it.

Female nurse 1: Okay.

Female nurse 2: Lie completely still now, so I don't hurt you. Yes, there you go. That's fine. We'll soon be done.

Female nurse 1: Is it Johan who is on duty tonight?

Female nurse 2: Yes, it is. Oh, dear! What…

Female nurse 1: Should I pull up?

Female nurse 2: Yes, otherwise she may fall out. Take it easy now, Eva-Lena. There is no danger. Try to relax.

Female nurse 3: What's going on?

Female nurse 2: She suddenly became uneasy.

Female nurse 3: Does she answer when spoken to?

Female nurse 2: No, not yet.

Female nurse 3: Hello! Do you hear me?

I: …

Female nurse 3: What's her name?

Female nurse 2: Eva-Lena.

Female nurse 3: Answer now, Eva-Lena! I know that you can hear me!

I: …

Female nurse 3: Can you look up now?

I: …

Female nurse 2: Shall we take her to room two then?

Female nurse 1: Yes, let's do that.

Female nurse 2: Eva-Lena?

I: …

Female nurse 1: She can't hear.

Female nurse 3: Can you calm down a bit now!

I: …

Female nurse 3: It's just as well that Johan comes and look at her. Calm down now, I said!

Female nurse 1: Should I call?

Female nurse 3: Yes, do that.

Female nurse 2: Just take it easy…

Female nurse 3: Yes, breath in this and try to calm down!

Female nurse 1: Can you come immediately?

Female nurse 3: Now, stop giving trouble and do as we say!

Female nurse 1: Yes, she is hyperventilating and uneasy… Yes… No… Okay.

Female nurse 3: Stop fooling around now!

Female nurse 2: Just breathe into the bag, and you'll soon feel better. That's it. You're doing well.

Female nurse 1: Johan is on his way.

Female nurse 2: Now she soon calms down.

Female nurse 3: This is nothing for us, but let him have a look at her before we send her on.

Ambulance guy 1: How's it going? Is she still not contactable?

Ambulance guy 2: No, it's unchanged.

Ambulance guy 1: I think it's wrong that we should transport psychiatric cases like this, when people who really need an ambulance may lie and die meanwhile.

Ambulance guy 2: Yes, but who would otherwise take care of them?

Ambulance guy 1: I don't know. Let them…

Ambulance guy 2: Watch what you're saying.

Ambulance guy 1: She doesn't hear.

Ambulance guy 2: Well, I think she does.

Ambulance guy 1: I just mean that I think it's rather unnecessary that we drive between the emergency department and Ulleråker like this. After all, we know that she isn't physically injured.

Ambulance guy 2: Yes, in principle I agree with you.

…

Ambulance guy 2: Did you see the fox?

Ambulance guy 1: What?

Ambulance guy 2: It was a fox that ran across the road.

Ambulance guy 1: Yeah?

Ambulance guy 1: Here we are.

Ambulance guy 2: Wait a minute, and I'll try to talk to her.

Ambulance guy 1: Yes, she should…

Ambulance guy 2: Hi. We've arrived now. Do you think you can raise and walk on your own?

I: …

Ambulance guy 2: Just sit up, and I'll help you down. That's it. How do you feel?

I: …

Ambulance guy 2: And here we climb down. Don't be afraid. I'm holding you. Grab my arm if you feel shaky. Is it going well?

I: …

Ambulance guy 2: Let's see now… Wait here, while I try to find out if there is someone here.

Male keeper: Hello. My name is Björn.

I: Hello.

He: You can come here with me.

I: …

He: How do you feel?

I: I don't know. I'm tired.

He: We can sit down and talk for a while if you like.

I: Can I buy cigarettes here some place?

He: No, but you can get some from me. Take as many as you want.

I: Thanks. I'll take two, then.

He: How do you feel?

I: I don't know.

He: Are you sad?

I: No. What time is it?

He: It's half past two.

I: …

He: Do you want to talk, or aren't you able to?

I: I don't know.

He: I don't mind listening.

I: But I don't know what to say. I just couldn't cross a bridge.

He: What bridge?

I: One in town. The one between Islandsbron and Nybron.

He: You mean Västgötaspången?

I: Yes.

He: Well, what happened there, then?

I: I got stuck.

He: In what way?

I: …

He: In what way did you get stuck?

I: I had been at the movies, and afterwards I stood on the bridge and smoked, and then I couldn't move away from there.

He: Why not?

I: Because I couldn't walk.

He: You couldn't?

I: No, I was like paralyzed.

He: Were you upset by the film, or what had happened?

I: I don't know. It was perhaps something with the film.

He: What kind of film was it?

I: I don't remember what it was called, but it was about a guy and a girl who were sexually obsessed with each other. You got to see how they had sex in different ways, and in the end the girl killed the guy while having sex and cut off his penis and put it in her vagina and went out into town with it in her, until the police came and took her.

He: I see.

I: Yes, but I didn't think it was especially upsetting. After all, it was just a film.

He: Mm… What happened next? When you stood on the bridge, I mean.

I: Someone came up to me and started to talk to me.

He: A guy?

I: Yes, or… I don't know how old he was, because I didn't see him.

He: You didn't?

I: No, I didn't look at him.

He: Why not?

I: I don't know.

He: But you talked with him?

I: Yes.

He: What did you talk about?

I: Why I stood there. He thought it was strange and asked if I wanted to take a walk with him.

He: But you didn't do that?

I: No, I couldn't walk.

He: No, sorry. What happened next?

I: Then he left, and I fell.

He: You fell? How did it happen?

I: I don't know.

He: What happened after that?

I: Then there was a crowd. First, two guys stopped and asked why I lay there, and then there was a crowd.

He: Yeah?

I: …

He: You fell on the bridge?

I: Yes, and then I got some kind of attack.

He: What kind of attack?

I: I began to breath rapidly, as if I didn't get any air.

He: It sounds like you began to hyperventilate.

I: Yes.

He: And this happened on Västgötaspången?
I: Yes.
He: And after that?
I: Then there was someone who called for an ambulance.
He: And then you came here?
I: No, first to the emergency department at Ackis and then here.
He: Yes, I see.
I: …
He: How do you feel now?
I: Tired.
He: Yes, I can understand that.
I: …
He: Do you think that what happened on the bridge was strange?
I: Yes.
He: Is there anything else you think is strange?
I: Yes.
He: Such as?
I: That I can take in others.
He: Take in?
I: Yes, I can think and feel as others. I can feel like anyone.
He: How do you explain that?
I: I don't know…
He: But you haven't always been able to do that?
I: No.
He: When did it start?

I: I don't know… This year.

He: And before? Was there something special that happened, or did it come sneaking in?

I: I don't know.

He: But you can take in other people's feelings and thoughts?

I: Yes.

He: …

I: You don't believe me, do you?

He: Yes, of course I do.

I: Yes, because otherwise I can tell you what you are feeling right now.

He: It's probably just as well that you get to talk with the doctor on duty…

I: Why?

He: To see if we can help you in some way… You don't mind, do you?

I: No…

He: If you come here with me then, we'll see if he's available.

Male doctor: My name is Schwarz. I'm doctor on duty here. Please sit down.

I: Thanks.

He: How do you feel?

I: I don't know.

He: You don't know?

I: No.

He: But something has happened?

I: …
He: Can you tell me what has happened?
I: …
He: Does it feel difficult?
I: …
He: Does it feel difficult to talk about it?
I: Yes.
He: But something isn't quite the way it usually is?
I: …
He: Is that correct?
I: Yes.
He: Can you tell me a little about it?
I: …
He: To Björn, whom you met earlier, you have said that you sometimes feel like other people. Is that right?
I: Yes…
He: How long have you had such feelings?
I: …
He: You don't want to talk about it?
I: No.
He: Why not?
I: Lasse also has one of those pens, and I know what that means!
He: Wait a minute, now. Like this you shouldn't… Come and sit down again.
I: …
He: You don't want to?
I: No.

He: Okay.

I: …

He: If you care to, you can stay here overnight, and we'll talk in the morning instead.

I: …

He: What do you think about that?

I: …

He: Shall we say so, that you stay here overnight, and then we'll see in the morning how it feels?

I: Yes…

He: Good. I'll ask Björn to show you to the ward.

The keeper: Did it go well?

I: No.

He: It didn't?

I: No, he was dumb!

He: In what way?

I: He didn't understand anything.

He: …

I: And he also had one of those pens that you hang around your neck in a string.

He: Yeah? Well, here we'll enter.

I: …

He: This is the admission ward.

I: …

He: Let's see now, if we can find an empty room…

I: …

He: Yes, in here you can sleep. Just inside the door here, there is a toilet.

I: …

He: How do you feel?

I: I don't know.

He: This is your bed.

I: Thanks.

He: Well, then…

I: It's light outside.

He: Yes. Do you want med to drop the blinds?

I: Yes, please.

He: Isn't there anyone at home who wonders where you are now?

I: I don't know.

He: You may call if you like. There is a telephone in the corridor outside.

I: Yes, it's probably just as well…

He: Do you have money?

I: Yes.

He: Meanwhile I'll go and fetch a toothbrush for you. I'll leave the door open so that you find your way back.

Lasse: Engström.

I: Hello, it's me.

He: Where the hell are you?!

I: I just want to tell you that I'll be gone for a few days now.

He: Are you with that fucking guy?

I: I'll be home in a few days then.

He: Go to hell!

I: I can't, because I'm already there.

He: What did you say?

I: No, it was nothing. I'll be home in a few days then. Bye-bye.

The keeper: Did it go well?

I: He asked me to go to hell.

He: He did?

I: Yes, but it doesn't matter.

He: Of course, it does.

I: …

He: I'll put the toothbrush here on the washbasin.

I: Thanks.

He: You may take off your clothes if you like.

I: Yes.

He: Okay. Do you think you can sleep now?

I: I don't know. Perhaps.

He: I'll leave the door ajar, and if there is anything you want, you know that we are here outside.

I: Yes.

He: Sleep well, then.

I: Thanks.

He: Bye-bye.

I: Bye.

…

I (sing quietly): "We'll manage this, both old and young, if we unite and spit in our fists."

Lasse called and wondered if I know where Eva-Lena is. She was supposed to go to the movies yesterday evening, and since then she is disappeared. No, not disappeared – at three o'clock in the morning she called him from somewhere and said that she would be gone for a few days. Lasse assumed that she was with "that fucking guy she runs after" and wondered what I thought. But I don't know what she is up to. The only thing I could say to him was that I don't think he needs to worry.

But afterwards I became a little hesitative, anyway. Can she really be with that guy? I thought. After all, he hasn't seemed especially interested in meeting her. And if she isn't with him – where is she then? But time will tell, I suppose.

This evening Lasse called again and asked if he could come over and talk for a while. He was worried about Eva-Lena and felt that her absence now, and her strange behaviour earlier, indicate that she is about to be mentally ill. She has, among other things, tried to drown herself in a water-butt and threatened to jump from the balcony, he said.

When he came here, I noticed that he was upset and needed to talk, so I listened to him without making any objections. Though certain things, like for instance that Eva-Lena is so confused that she walks around somewhere now and can't take care of herself, I couldn't agree with. Because I don't think it is that way, even though I can't know for sure.

And finally, he calmed down and came up with some other subjects. But he didn't stay for so long, and before he left he hugged me and thanked me for listening.

Female doctor: Hello, my name is Ingegerd Axelsson and I'm a doctor here. This is contact person Evy.

I: Hello.

She: We are here to talk with you a little about how you feel, if you don't mind?

I: No, it's okay.

She: How do you feel today?

I: I don't know.

She: But on Friday night it was difficult?

I: Yes…

She: Can you tell us what happened?

I: …

She: What was it, that caused you to come here?

I: That I couldn't walk.

She: You couldn't walk?

I: No.

She: How come?

I: I don't know.

She: Do you think it's difficult to talk about it?

I: Yes.

She: What had you done earlier in the evening?

I: Been at the movies.

She: And then?

I: Then I couldn't come home.

She: You collapsed on the street?

I: Yes.

She: And what happened then?

I: People came up to me and wondered why I lay there.

She: And what did you answer to that?

I: Nothing.

She: Nothing at all?

I: No, I couldn't talk. They wondered if I were an epileptic or if I were drunk or if I had taken drugs, but I couldn't answer.

She: How was it then? Had you taken something?

I: No.

She: No alcohol and no narcotics?

I: No!

She: Well, you may understand that I must ask…

I: …

She: Have you been involved with something like that before?

I: What?

She: That you haven't been able to move?

I: Yes, but not like that.

She: Not as marked as on Friday night?

I: No.

She: Have you felt for long, that something has been different compared to previously?

I: I don't know… Half a year perhaps.

She: Half a year. And what is it that hasn't been quite the same?

I: It's perhaps that I…

She: You haven't quite recognized yourself?

I: No…

She: Can you describe in what way you have felt different?

I: …

She: Have you been nervous, uneasy, felt anxiety?

I: Anxiety? What's that?

She: Have you felt sad then, more than previously?

I: Yes, but it doesn't matter.

She: You don't mind feeling that way?

I: No.

She: Have you been more tired also, and more in-active?

I: Yes, I lie down on my bed as soon as I can and have no desire to do the things I should.

She: Such as…?

I: Such as shop, prepare food and clean.

She: You are married?

I: Yes.

She: What does your husband say then, about your changed behaviour?

I: He thinks I'm crazy.

She: Why?

I: I don't know.

She: How is your relationship otherwise?

I: Bad. I don't want to be married to him anymore.

That's why he's angry.

She: He doesn't want you to divorce him?

I: No.

She: But you want a divorce?

I: Yes.

She: Can you tell me why?

I: Yes, because I have fallen in love with another.

She: Whom you have started a relationship with?

I: No.

She: Why do you laugh?

I: …

She: You haven't started a new relationship, but your husband knows that you have met another?

I: Yes.

She: And this other man… Do you meet him sometimes or…?

I: No, not any longer. We worked at the same place, but he has quit now.

She: He was, in other words, a work mate of yours?

I: Yes, you could say that.

She: And your feelings for him have caused you to want to break up of marriage?

I: Yes, because now I understand that… my husband has never seen me as I really am.

She: But this other man does, you think?

I: Yes.

She: Do you have feelings of guilt about this, or how do you experience it?

I: No, why should I feel guilty?

She: You don't?

I: No, you can't help what you feel. At first I thought it wouldn't lead to me wanting a divorce, but now I think it's just fine that I have realized that I don't want to be married to him anymore. Whatever happens, I don't want to continue being married to him.

She: You mean that even if the other man should say no to you, you don't want to continue your marriage?

I: Yes, that's what I mean.

She: Have you talked about this together, you and your husband?

I: No, but I know that he doesn't want to divorce. He loves me, he says. But if he did, I think he would like to help me to be free, instead of trying to put me down. He doesn't care about what I think and is satisfied as long as I don't protest. It makes no difference to him that I don't love him, only he can continue to… Why does he want to go on being married to me, though he knows that I'm interested in another and don't want him? I don't understand that.

She: But you still have sexual intimacy?

I: No, it's no intimacy.

She: What do you mean by that?

I: I mean that he tries to force himself on me against my will! He doesn't care about what I want. I have tried to talk with him, and I have threatened to call out to the neighbors, or to call the police, but nothing has helped.

She: He has insisted?

I: Yes, and I don't understand why.

She: Have you called home and told him what has happened now?

I: No, I haven't.

She: Why not?

I: Because I don't think it's any of his business.

She: He doesn't know that you're here?

I: No, I called home Friday night and told him that I won't be coming home for a while, and he took it for granted that I was with... the other, and I let him believe that.

She: How did he react to it?

I: He got angry. Go to hell! he shouted and slammed the receiver down.

She: I see... Well, then I just want to hear a little about what you yourself think about this.

I: I don't know...

She: But you don't mind staying here for a while?

I: No, I don't want to go home and fight.

 She: You think you can't handle the situation as it is at home right now?

I: No, I need to be on my own and think.

She: But you don't want to tell your husband where you are?

I: No.

She: Why not?

I: No, because if he believes that I am with... the other, then he'll perhaps realize that I'm serious when I say that I want a divorce.

She: Well, let's conclude our conversation here and wait a few days… Do we agree on that?
I: Yes.
She: Okay. Goodbye then, until we meet again.
I: Goodbye.

Eva-Lena hasn't tried to get in touch with me. I called Lasse and asked how it was, and he said that she still has neither phoned nor come home. He wondered if I thought that he should turn to the police.

But if she said that she would come home again in a few days, she probably will. I advised him to wait. The police wouldn't do anything about it anyway. But I understand that he is anxious, because now even I begin to wonder what she's up to.

Male keeper: Are you sitting here all by yourself?
I: Yes.
He: Wouldn't you rather watch TV with the others?
I: No.
He: No, the children's program may not be so funny…
ny…
I: …
He: How do you feel?
I: I don't know…
He: Are you sad?
I: Yes.

He: Why?

I: I'm not really allowed to say this, but separately I don't understand what I have to do here.

He: Separately?

I: Yes, but it's me who has let it happen, so I'm not entitled to complain.

He: Are you afraid?

I: No, but it feels strange. I have never been in a place like this before.

He: …

I: But I might as well be here as elsewhere. I don't have to be ashamed.

He: No, why should you be ashamed?

I: Here there isn't anyone who hates me all the time, anyway.

He: …

I: I can't manage to exert myself anymore.

He: With what?

I: With trying to keep up appearances, and to be on guard, and to defend myself against all physical and psychical attacks.

He: Who's attacking you?

I: My husband.

He: But then it's perhaps restful to be here for a while?

I: Yes, because I can't take any more. I must come away from him.

He: …

I: He hates me, but he still wants to be married to

me and live with me and have sex with me. I don't understand that. And he threatens me all the time… I'm not afraid of him, but it's so exhausting never to be left alone.

He: Yes, I understand that.

I: Do you? You don't believe I say all this because I'm nuts then?

He: What do you mean?

I: I could come up with this just to avoid admitting that I'm crazy.

He: I don't believe you're crazy.

I: But if I claimed that I'm completely sound and shouldn't really be here, you would probably take it as an indication that I'm so sick that I lack disease awareness.

He: No, I don't think so. Why is he nasty to you?

I: Because I want a divorce. But that's not the problem.

He: What's the problem then?

I: That I can feel everything.

He: What do you mean by everything?

I: Everything that exists. It feels so burdensome and overwhelming… I don't know how to sort it out. But I must do it, because otherwise I'll never be free.

He: What is it that you must sort out, then?

I: Why it happened and why I'm here.

He: What happened before you got here, you mean?

I: Yes.

He: …

I: How can you be free of something that is neither understandable with reason nor with feelings?

He: I don't know…

I: But it's nothing to talk about. I have to manage myself. I just wish that I knew better how to do it.

Eva-Lena is at Ulleråker. She called today and told me. But she still hasn't called Lasse, and she made me promise not to tell him, if he should ask if I've heard from her. We talked just briefly, because she rang from the pay telephone at the hospital, and there were several others who were waiting to call. I got to know that she went to Ulleråker by ambulance on Friday night but nothing more. What had happened before that, she didn't say.

When we talked, she sounded almost normal, and she didn't believe that she had to stay much longer at the hospital. I will probably get to know better what she has been up to when she comes home. What worries me the most just now, is how I'll be able to avoid telling Lasse that I have heard from her, if he should call again.

Male keeper: We haven't met, have we? Hello. My name is Bosse, and I work nights at this ward.

I: Hello.

He: Have you recently arrived here?

I: Yes.

He: Shall we go and sit down somewhere and talk a

little to get to know each other?

I: Well…

He: If you care to, that is?

I: Okay.

He: Let's see where we can be… In the ward kitchen perhaps, it should be empty this time of day. If you'll come here with me…

I: …

He: Would you like me to turn on the ceiling lamp or do you prefer to sit in the dark?

I: I don't know.

He: Sometimes I think it's easier to talk if it isn't too light.

I: Yes.

He: We don't need to sit at the table either, if we don't want to. That can easily be too formal.

I: …

He: We'll sit here on the floor, I think. What do you say about that?

I: Okay…

He: Fine. My name is Bosse, as I said, and I work as a keeper here.

I: Eva-Lena.

He: Hi.

I: …

He: The first thing I noticed about you, was your eyes. You have very beautiful and expressive eyes.

I: Thanks.

He: I fell for them immediately.

I: And I fell for your voice.

He: You did? Yes, the first impression is important. Sometimes it can be completely decisive for the continuing.

I: Yes.

He: But I'm afraid of getting engaged too deeply.

I: You are?

He: Yes.

I: Why?

He: Because I think it's frightening to let emotions take over. And I'm also afraid of becoming bound.

I: I'm not. I think that you become freer the more you feel.

He: Yes, but opening can be painful sometimes.

I: Let it be that way then! You can't let yourself be held back by that. You must be open.

He: Yes…

I: And if you're not able to be, you should find out what it is that is holding you back.

He: I see… And how do you do that?

I: You should know that, since you're working at a place like this!

He: No, tell me.

I: You must stop defending yourself.

He: Against what?

I: Against the pain. You must feel it, instead of defending yourself against it.

He: And how can that be done?

I: You should, for instance, not take a cigarette to

suppress it, or have an anger outburst to avoid feeling it. Instead you should open yourself to it and let yourself be filled up by it and just *be* it. And when you feel it, you get to know to what and to whom it was connected from the beginning.

He: From the beginning?

I: Yes, it's a pain from your childhood that awakens. But when you feel it, you get to know in what way your parents let you down, and what you did to avoid the knowledge that you weren't loved.

He: I see.

I: Yes, you must feel how it is connected, so that you can open and experience the present. Otherwise, you are controlled and blocked by the unexperienced pain and avoid, for instance, to engage in deeper relationships.

He: Like I do, you mean?

I: Yes.

He: Mm… Is this something you apply in your own life, or is it only theoretical reasoning?

I: I apply it.

He: And it works?

I: Yes. Everything can be adjusted, if you're just prepared for it.

I opened to my beloved, but my beloved had turned and gone. My soul failed me when he spoke. I sought him, but found him not; I called him, but he gave no answer. The watchmen found me, as they went about in the city; they beat me, they wounded me, they took away my mantle those watchmen of the walls. I adjure you, O daughters of Jerusalem, if you find my beloved that you tell him I am sick with love. (Song of Solomon 5:6-8)

Male patient: What are you doing, Eva-Lena?
   I: I'm looking out.
   He: What do you see?
   I: An ambulance.
   He: Are they coming with another one?
   I: Yes, I think so.
   He: …
   I: This is the place where they bring all the nutcases they have cleared away from the streets.
   He: Yes.
   I: You're not permitted to lie outdoors and make it untidy.
   He: No. Do you see the moon?
   I: Yes.
   He: Do you see the bloody moon above the tree-tops you fucking maid? as the farm-hand said, trying to be romantic.
   I: Yes… How did you get here?
   He: What do you mean?
   I: Did you come with a police car or an ambulance?
   He: I got a lift from the cops.
   I: Were you drunk?

He: No, not really.

I: Why did you get to ride with the cops then? Had you had a fight?

He: No, but behaved a little unsuitable, maybe.

I: Yes, you aren't permitted to do that.

He: No, because then you will be locked up in the madhouse.

I: Yes. Have you been here long?

He: No, I came here last week.

I: How long must you stay?

He: I don't know. As long as I want.

I: Have you been here before?

He: Yes, a few times.

I: …

He: You don't have permission to go out, have you?

I: I don't know.

He: Haven't they told you?

I: No.

He: If there is anything you need from the kiosk, just let me know.

I: Thanks.

He: Are you longing out?

I: No.

He: Is something happening down there?

I: No, not any longer.

He: Come here and sit next to me, then.

I: …

He: Do you want some juice?

I: Yes, please.

…

He: Here you'll see… A first-rate grog with vodka and orange juice!

I: Thanks.

He: Do you like vodka?

I: Yes.

He: Cheers then, and welcome here!

I: Thanks.

He: May I possibly offer the young lady a cigarette also?

I: Yes, please.

…

I: Why do you knit on that scarf that you usually sit with during the day?

He: Because it's relaxing. And there's a lot that has to do with sexuality…

I: Yes.

…

He: Do you feel the booze yet?

I: Yes, I'll soon be drunk.

He: Oh, what slender shoulders!

I: Bony, you mean?

He: Yes, bony, ha, ha.

…

I: Are you afraid of having sex with women?

He: What?

I: Are you afraid of having sex with women?

He: Why are you asking that?

I: Because I want to know. Are you?

He: Yes, sometimes maybe…

I: But you don't have to be.

He: No?

I: No. If you come with me to my room, I'll show you that you don't have to be afraid.

He: What will we do there?

I: You'll see when we get there.

He: Shit, I get upset when you talk like that!

I: Why?

He: Well, what do you think?

I: I don't know. I just want to show you that you don't have to be afraid.

He: In that case, I want to know how it will happen.

I: No, I can't say, because I won't know before we are there and let it be what it must be.

He: What do you mean by that?

I: The way it becomes when you follow what you feel, I mean.

He: No, now I must have another grog! Shall I make one for you, too?

I: Yes, please.

…

He: Here you are.

I: Thanks. Where are all the others?

He: Asleep, I guess.

I: Yes, it's only you and me here.

He: Mm.

I: I like you.

He: And I like you. Let's toast to that!

...

I: Are you drunk?

He: A little. Are you?

I: Yes. Shall we go to the room, then?

He: No, I don't dare.

I: Why not?

He: Because I think I know what you want to do.

I: I just want to show you that you don't have to be afraid.

He: Yeah… right. I become so upset that I think I must go and get my medications ahead of schedule.

I: No, it's not necessary.

He: It isn't?

I: No, we don't have to do it. We can sit here and drink only. In that case you aren't afraid, are you?

He: No, in that case I feel calm.

I: We just sit here.

He: Yes, you and me and the bloody moon.

I have been to mamma. I think it was so dumb that she, who has bad lungs, should move to the central city after the divorce to live in the middle of the exhaust and all shit, while papa stayed in the apartment. She should of course have remained there, and papa could have moved to town instead. It was so idiotic!

In the beginning, she visited acquaintances or took a taxi out to a forest hill and sat there for a few hours, but when she got worse, she couldn't do that anymore. She had to take more and more oxygen, and now she is forced to have it all the time, twenty-four hours a day.

At home she has one gas cylinder in the bedroom, and one in the kitchen with long tubes, so that she can walk around in the apartment. And when she goes out, she has a little oxygen cylinder in a shopping cart that she can take with her, because if she doesn't take any oxygen, she gets respiratory distress and becomes cyanotic.

She can never feel really free. Because at the same time as she has become worse physically, she has got mentally broken down by being so restricted in not being able to do what she wants.

Female doctor: Hello. My name is Barbro Westerberg. I'm a consultant here at the hospital. You have already met Ingegerd, if I've got it right?

I: Yes.

She: Well, we would like to hear a little about how you feel now.

I: …

She: Do you feel better, or is it about the same as before?

I: About the same.

She: You feel nervous and uneasy?

I: Yes, sometimes.

She: But you have no feelings of unreality?

I: No…

She: You sound uncertain?

I: I don't feel unreal, but it is as if I am in several different ways.

She: You don't quite recognize yourself?

I: No, not all the time.

She: Are you worried about that this could mean that you have… schizophrenia?

I: No, why should I be worried about that?

She: You aren't afraid?

I: No, not about that, anyway.

She: But there are other things you are afraid of?

I: No.

She: How long have it been like this?

I: Half a year perhaps. Since I became aware.

She: Aware of what?

I: Of everything possible.

She: Such as, for example?

I: That I want a divorce.

She: Yes, your husband… You still haven't called him and told him where you are?

I: No.

She: You don't think it would be a good idea to let him come here, in order to discuss this in the presence of a third person?

I: No, I don't. It's enough that I'm allowed to be here.

She: But shouldn't you try to work through your problems, instead of just go and wait for the solution to come flying by itself?

I: I don't believe it will come flying! You may think that I'm here just to be lazy, but I'm not!

She: No, it was only a suggestion. But if you don't think that…

I: No, I don't!

She: You are completely convinced that you want to divorce?

I: Yes, I am!

She: And you are aware that a divorce can implicate big emotional stresses?

I: Yes, but you can't continue to be married to a person that you don't want to live with, just to avoid stresses! That's perhaps what *you* would do, but not me!

She: But you haven't turned in a divorce application yet?

I: No.

She: Why not?

I: Because I want us to part as friends.

She: And that's impossible right now?

I: Yes.

She: What are you in disagreement about?

I: He is angry because I'm in love with someone else.

She: But you don't meet this other man anymore, if I've got it right?

I: No.

She: So now it's more of an infatuation from a distance?

I: No. It might seem like that, but it isn't. Rather the opposite.

She: What do you mean by that?

I: That he feels as close all the same.

She: You think you're close to him?

I: Yes.

She: But nothing spoken of has happened between you?

I: No.

She: He's perhaps also married?

I: No, he isn't.

She: Well, then… How do you look at this that you have got into? What are your thoughts about it?

I: I don't know…

She: Have you had any mental problems earlier in your life, or is this the first time?

I: This is the first time.

She: Do you think it's difficult to talk about it?

I: Why do ask that?

She: I just get an impression that you don't like to talk about yourself.

I: In that case, I never do.

She: You're always a bit secretive about yourself?

I: Yes. And I don't know what you want to know.

She: Well, I can ask, for example, if you have heard any voices.

I: What kind of voices?

She: Voices within you that, for example, encourage you to do different things… Do you recognize that?

I: No… Or it doesn't matter.

She: You don't think it matters? But if we shall be able to help you in the best way, it's important that we

get to know as much as possible about how you feel.
You certainly understand that?

I: Yes, but I have nothing more to say.

Now Eva-Lena has called Lasse and told him that she is at Ulleråker. He came by for a while yesterday evening and wanted to hear what I think of it.

First, he asked if she has called me also, and I said – what was true – that she has, but I didn't tell him when.

Then he said that he thinks that Eva-Lena is schizophrenic. But I couldn't agree with that. I couldn't – can't – deny that I think she has changed, but going so far as to claim that she is mentally ill, I can't do.

And he asked me what she has said to me about Johan. I told him a little, at the same time as I had to admit that I don't understand all her thoughts and reflections about him.

So here we sat, almost as in the good old days, and worried about her! I almost burst out laughing when I thought of it.

Male patient 1: Play something on the piano, Rolle, to cheer us up! Take that song Lill Lindfors usually sings.

Male patient 2: What song does she sing then?

Male patient 1: This one, you know (starts to sing) "You are the only one who secretly sees me, though no one has spoken you know what I ask you…"

Male patient 2: (starts to play the piano).

Male patient 1: Yes, that's the one!

Female keeper: Shall I help you Hilma?

Male patient 3: …requires models that contribute with common interpretation courses which can be the basis for…

Male patient 1 (sings): "…my fate is to be yours, in my fantasy to share the world that is yours."

Male patient 4: …Nybron and Islandsbron. No, let's see… There is another one between them… What's that walking bridge with flower boxes called?

Male patient 5: Västgötaspången?

Male patient 4: Yes, that's the one. If you choose one of those bridges, and then walk…

Male patient 1: Shit! What's happening to *her* now, all of a sudden?

Male patient 4: Can you come here for a while? The chick on the sofa here doesn't seem to feel very well.

Female keeper: Fredrik! Fetch Anders and come quickly and take care of Eva-Lena!

Male patient 4: It was a devil to go on!

Female patient: No, no, no!

Female keeper: Take it easy, Rosa, it's nothing to be afraid of.

Female patient: But what if she dies!

Female keeper: No, she won't die.

Male patient 4: Does she practice physiotherapy?

Female patient: Why does she sound like that? Why

is she acting this way?

Female keeper: This will soon blow over. Don't look if you think it's scary.

Male patient 1: Shit!

Female patient: Is she sick? Is she choking?

Female keeper: No, you don't need to be scared.

Male patient 4: Do something damn it, or are you going to let her break her neck?

Female keeper: Now Fredrik and Anders are coming to help her. Do you see that, Rosa?

Female patient: Yes. What are they going to do with her?

Female keeper: They'll take her to her room and let her lie down on her bed and rest a little. There's no danger, Rosa.

Female patient: I was so afraid…

Female keeper: Yes, but now it's over.

Female patient: Is she dead?

Female keeper: No, she isn't.

Female patient: Why do they carry her away, then?

Lasse has called the hospital and made inquiries about Eva-Lena. He was told by one of the doctors, that they are convinced that she is moving into a psychotic state now, and that she probably will need medication to come out of it. But they were not certain that she would like to stay at the hospital of her own free will, and therefore the doctor asked Lasse if he were willing to sign an app-

lication of admittance for care. They wanted her to be taken into compulsory care, that is. And he agreed.

Female keeper: How are you, Eva-Lena? Why are you standing here?

I: I'm waiting for the rounds to come out. There was something I forget to ask when they were in my room.

Female keeper: I see. They'll be here in a minute. Yes, here they come now.

I: Excuse me for interrupting, but there was something I forgot to ask.

Male doctor: Yes?

I: I just wonder if I can be permitted to go home soon.

The doctor: You want to go home?

I: Yes.

The doctor: How do you feel then? Do you feel better now, you think?

I: Yes.

The doctor: But you are a little tired?

I: No, I'm not tired.

The doctor: Do you feel dizzy then?

I: No.

The doctor: You're able to stand up?

I: Yes.

Female keeper: Stand up now, Eva-Lena.

The doctor: You're able to stand?

I: Yes, but you are so many, and I'm only one...

Female keeper: Come on, Eva-Lena. I'll help you up.

…

Female keeper: Are you steady now?

I: Yes, I'm fine. Can I go home then?

The doctor: Well, it will probably be best if you stay here a few more days… Don't you think so?

I: …

The doctor: We'll wait with discharge until you feel a little stronger. Don't you agree?

I: Yes.

The doctor: Bye, then.

I: Bye.

I freeze and feel ill. I hope I'm not getting sick. I feel something in my stomach also, about the way I did when I got salpingitis. It was at the same time as it was about to end between Bosse and me.

We had been out in the country all day, and in the evening we went to Bosse's brother, who was turning forty, and then I felt so tired. The next day, when I was at work, there was suddenly a sharp pain in my belly. A doctor who was standing nearby, saw that I turned completely pale grey in my face and was about to pass out, so I was sent to lie down on a bunk in a treatment room and rest. I felt totally finished, but I struggled on at work anyway, as good as I could.

Before I should go home, the doctor asked me how I felt. "If your fever goes high, you had better go to the hos-

pital," he said and wrote out a referral, in case I should be forced to go there.

And I lay at home and had middle high fever and didn't know how to do. I stayed in bed the whole weekend, and then I went to work on Monday and got a sedimentation test. And it was completely too high, so the doctor sent me to the hospital, where they suspected salpingitis, and I was admitted and got penicillin.

Eva-Lena is home again. She called yesterday evening and told me. But she couldn't speak freely, so we decided to catch up another evening instead. It's good anyway that nothing came of that compulsory care, that there was some talk of before.

I still feel out of sorts, but I have worked as usual.

Yesterday Eva-Lena called again. She is busy writing down what happened in connection with her winding up in hospital, and I think that's fine, because it can serve as an adaption at the same time.

After the movies she had collapsed on a bridge in town and was taken with some kind of attack. She thinks it happened because she had been emotionally affected by something in the film – which was a lot about sex. At the same time, she had the feeling that it wasn't about herself but about Johan. She said that it was for his sake she let *it happen and went along with being taken to Ulleråker.*

Well, I don't know what to think about that. But it's fine that she is home again. Even the doctor who discharged her, had said that it wasn't good for her to stay in hospital, so evidently her condition wasn't as bad as they assumed from the beginning.

Lasse: Now we'll do it from behind!

I: No, we won't! How many times do I have to tell you that I don't want to?

He: But you don't have to do anything. Just turn around, and I'll take care of the rest.

I: No, I'm going to sleep now!

He: Yes, you can sleep while I fuck you.

I: I don't want to, I said! Why can't you get it? I'll *never* want to do it again, so you can find someone else to lay now.

He: And who the hell should that be? One of your little girlfriends, maybe?

I: You can meet someone on your own.

He: That isn't so fucking easy.

I: Fix it for yourself then!

He: So while you lie here and are horny for someone else, I'm supposed to stand in the bathroom and jack off, you mean?

I: Yes, to do that, must be better than forcing yourself on another with violence anyway!

He: We are married, damn it!

I: And that means that you have the right to behave just as you like? Besides, we shall divorce.

He: That hasn't happened yet.

I: You don't believe me?

He: Forget it! Take of your panties now and let's fuck!

I: No, I said!

He: …

I: Do you have difficulty getting it?

He: …

I: Let go! You're pulling them apart!

He: Take them off then!

I: No, I won't!

He: You fucking little…

I: Are you out of your mind? Now you have to pay for them!

He: Who's really insane here? I would be fucking careful talking like that if I were in your shoes!

I: But why must you carry on like this? Why can't you just accept that I don't want to and leave me alone?

He: Because I love you!

I: No, you don't! You don't know me, and you never have.

He: I know your cunt.

I: Take your hand away!

He: …

I: The only thing you care about is sex. That's why you could lie with anyone. But I'm not just a body!

And when you say you love me you lie, because you don't know what love is!

He: But you do, you mean?

I: I'm beginning to understand what it's *not* anyway.

He: Stop fussing now and lay still!

I: I'm not fussing! And if you don't let go I'll scream.

He: But with the whippersnapper it would be just fine, wouldn't it? You wouldn't mind fucking him! Too bad that the interest doesn't seem to be mutual, then!

I: You know nothing about that!

He: I don't? Why are you still here, then?

I: …

He: I know a lot fucking more than you think!

I: Good for you, then! But now I'm going to sleep.

Lasse called. He doesn't think that Eva-Lena has gotten better since she was at Ulleråker. Rather the opposite, because now she has evidently threatened him with a carving-knife also. He said that it would perhaps have been better if they had kept her in hospital a bit longer, and that she had gone through a proper medical treatment.

"Well, medicines," I said – because I don't believe in medication at all for mental problems – "they just use to drug people in places like that."

Yes, but like this he couldn't have it any longer, he declared. He couldn't find a moment's peace.

And of course I can understand that it must be difficult for him to not know if he can rely on Eva-Lena. But at the same time, I think that he must have confidence in her and her own ability to solve her problems.

Though I didn't say that. I find myself in such a diffi-cult middle position when he turns to me with his trou-bles with her, because at the same time as I know I must accept his anxiety, I don't think it's really justified. But that conviction I can't convey to him.

Unknown guy: Would you like something to drink?
I: Yes, please. But I'm already drunk. Are you drunk?
He: No, not really.
I: What have you done tonight?
He: Been at a party. What have you done?
I: Been with a friend. That's where I drank. Then I met you.
He: Yes, I knew that something would happen this evening. I had a feeling of it already when I went out.
I: But don't you think I'm too old?
He: Nope.
I: …
He: What's your name?
I: Eva-Lena. What's yours?
He: Johan.
I: Are you called Johan?
He: Yes. What's so funny?
I: I just came to think of something… What's this?

He: Vodka and lime.

I: Yes, I'm familiar with that.

He: …

I: You don't possibly have a cigarette also?

He: Certainly. Here you are. Take as many as you want.

I: That's what he said, too.

He: Who?

I: Why did you come up to me in the street?

He: I don't know… Why did you embrace me?

I: Because it felt like it.

He: It was in the same way for me.

I: But didn't you think it was strange that I hugged you just like that?

He: No, not really.

…

I: There is no ashtray here.

He: No, but you can put your ashes in my glass here.

I: Everything is symbolic.

He: It is?

I: Yes, everything has a double meaning.

He: What do you mean by that?

I: It *may* have, anyway.

He: Yes, but how?

I: If you say that I may put my ashes in your glass, it means not only that I may put ashes there, but also something more that has to do with our emotional relationship.

He: Yeah?

I: Yes, it does, but I can't explain how it works.

He: No, that's okay.

I: You're kind. I like you.

He: And I like you.

I: You do? Don't you think I'm nuts then?

He: No, why would I think that?

I: Because I drink too much and say strange things.

He: No, I don't think so. But put out that one now, and let's go to bed.

I: Mm… That's why you wanted me to come home with you, wasn't it?

He: Partly.

I: But haven't you, who are so good-looking, a girlfriend who you can fuck?

He: No, unfortunately not.

I: But you don't even know me.

He: Well, enough to know that I like you, anyway.

I: Yes, that's something you know almost at once.

He: Come and lie down now, before you fall off the chair.

I: Yes, here I come… Oh, dear!

He: Yes, watch your head.

I: Yes.

He: Are you comfortable?

I: I don't know. Everything is spinning. The bed is spinning.

He: It will soon be better.

I: It will?

He: Yes, soon I'll come and hold you.

...

I: There isn't any plastic on this bed.

He: Plastic?

I: Yes, under the sheet. Every time I moved in bed the plastic rustled.

He: ...

I: I didn't have a nightgown, so I got to sleep in my bra and panties.

He: Yes, but here with me you can sleep naked.

I: Yes.

...

I: I can't see anything.

He: Why not?

I: Because it's totally dark.

He: ...

I: When I was little I had a black patch over one eye. I was cross-eyed and should be forced to train up my sight in the bad eye that I had disconnected to avoid seeing the truth.

He: ...

I (sing): "I'm a Lapp and I have my reindeer, I've the troll drum's rhythm in my blood." (stop singing). No, this is how it goes (start to sing) "I am slack because I've drunk spirits, I've the troll drink's poison in my blood..." (stop singing). What are you doing?

He: I'm getting undressed.

I: Why?

He: You know why.

I: Yes, so that we can fuck.

He: Yes, and now it's your turn.

I: …

He: You're aware of what I'm doing?

I: Yes, you're taking off my clothes. You're undressing me because I can't do it myself.

He: Yes, and now I'm coming to lie down with you.

I: Yes.

He: Hi.

I: You're heavy. I can't breathe.

He: Better this way?

I: Yes.

He: What are you thinking of?

I: Do you know that you're selling your soul now?

He: I am?

I: Yes, you're selling your soul for your body.

He: Mm.

I: Doesn't that bother you?

He: What do you mean?

I: That you're selling your soul?

He: No. Well, yes. Ah… I don't know.

I: Why don't you know?

He: It feels so strange. It feels as if I both want to, and don't want to.

I: Why don't you know?

He: I don't know.

I: But I know.

He: No, wait! Where are you going?

I: …

He: What are you doing?

I: Getting dressed.

He: Why?

I: Because I'm leaving.

He: Why?

I: Because I have to.

He: Why do you have to?

I: Because I'll never deny you, Johan! Whatever happens, I will never deny you.

Upon my bed by night I sought him whom my soul loves; I sought him, but found him not; I called him, but he gave no answer. "I will rise now and go about the city, in the streets and in the squares; I will seek him whom my soul loves." I sought him but found him not. (Song of Solomon 3:1-2)

I hope that what Eva-Lena has been involved in, has influenced her in the right direction, because otherwise there is a risk that she shall get stuck in something that leads nowhere. I don't doubt that she will succeed in getting through it, because I know how determined she is to get to the bottom of her problems – in contrast to certain others in my life! – but the question is how long it will take.

Once when mamma, Anita, and I were in the country, mamma began to talk about how it was for her when she was little. Her papa died when she was six years old, and we understood that it wasn't always very easy for her and her brother to live with grandmother.

Now I can't remember what it was that made her so upset, but I know that she sat in the hammock when it happened. She sat there and swayed to and fro, and suddenly she said: "Oh, it's so terrible!" She was completely upset and seemed to remember something that had happened to her many years ago. Anita and I let her be, because we realized that she had come into a feeling. We just stayed by her side so that she could feel safe while it happened. And I thought it was so good, of course, that she had come into something.

But she was probably not strong enough to manage experiencing all of it, for after a while she shut down and absolutely wanted her pills. She lay down on the bed and took a Sobril, though Anita and I tried as long as possible to get her to refrain, so that she could come back into the feeling.

But she couldn't manage it, and I thought it was such a shame, because I regarded it as she had had a chance to come to an understanding, which might have made her freer.

It wasn't Anita and I that had forced her to remember. She had talked herself into the memory and the feeling on her own. But not so long after that, we got to see a newspaper clipping on her refrigerator door where you could read that everyone has the right to keep a lifelong deception, and then both Anita and I felt that it was directly addressed to us.

And then I thought: How can she choose that? Even if it's tough, don't you always want to know the truth? That she deliberately deselected the truth, was an even bigger disappointment to me than that she hadn't been able to feel everything at once. She could have returned to it on a later occasion, I thought. But she didn't intend to do that. Instead it ended with her deciding that she would avoid the truth for ever.

Kicki: Would you like some more tea?

I: No thanks.

She: But I'll have another cup, I think.

I: I wish I knew why I wound up at Ulleråker.

She: Yes, but don't you?

I: No, not really. "Afterwards one is wise, said Carlander, was released from the madhouse!" But I don't know. Everything feels so heavy and overwhelming… I almost don't manage to bear it. And when I happen to pass Västgötaspången or see an ambulance, there is a twinge in me, and I think: It's so terrible! But that's not my opinion.

She: You mean that it's someone else who thinks like that?

I: Yes, that's how it feels, anyway. So, it possibly isn't for me it's tough that I have been to Ulleråker, either.

She: How many days were you there?

I: Twelve. First, I was at the admission ward for five days, and then at the treatment ward for seven.

She: How was it?

I: Well, it was good, I suppose… In the beginning I wasn't allowed to go out, but I didn't want to either, so it didn't matter.

She: You were at a locked ward, that is?

I: Yes, but I had a bed to sleep in, and I got food to eat, and I didn't need more, I thought. And it was comfortable to be in a place where you could do what you felt without having to worry about if it were appropriate or not.

She: Mm… What did you do during the day, then?

I: Nothing special. There was a ping-pong table, a piano, playing cards, puzzles, radio, TV, books, and a therapy unit, but I just… I don't know what they did in therapy, because I was never there. Once I played cards with some patients and keepers, and once I helped an old lady to sort out pieces for a puzzle that she tried to solve, but mostly I just sat on the sofa in the day room and smoked.

She: You didn't read anything, then?

I: No, I couldn't concentrate on that. Once I looked at the books, but I didn't borrow anything. Well, I took the Bible, but not to read it, but to look for something that I could send to Johan. At first, I didn't know if I should dare to write to him from the hospital, because I didn't want them to find out his name and address, but then I thought that if it wasn't possible for them to phone Lasse without my permission, they couldn't contact Johan either. They must follow the professional secrecy, as you know. But they never found out, because I asked a guy, who had permission to go out, to post the letter for me instead.

She: Did you talk with someone about your problems, then?

I: Yes, there were a couple of doctors who came and questioned me. But I didn't feel any confidence in them. I didn't tell them, for instance, that I can identify with Johan. I know that I do, but I don't believe it's generally accepted that it's possible. If that were the case, you would have heard about it or read about it somewhere.

She: Mm.

I: I know there is something that's called *folie à deux,* which is a kind of mental illness that is transmitted from one person to another through strong feelings, such as love for instance, but I don't know if that's what I have.

She: What did the doctors say, then?

I: Nothing. Though I didn't ask for their opinion, either. They didn't know what was wrong with me, I suppose. I believed that they should try to find out, but they didn't. They didn't ask me anything about my childhood and parents. And I didn't get any medication or any therapy. I was just permitted to be there. They perceived perhaps that it wasn't I who was sick. I think and feel strange things sometimes, but I have control over it all the time, so I can't think that I'm sick. After all, I'm the one who decides.

She: What strange things are you thinking?

I: Well, what should I say… The strangest is probably that I think that people talk about completely different things than they are aware of themselves. They communicate with each other on a deeper level by, for instance, discussing the weather, and that symbolic language I can interpret now. As soon as I feel that what is being said is upsetting, I understand the underlying meaning. I can't explain how it happens. Suddenly I just know that a potted plant means an embryo, and that mittens are the same as children. I never thought and felt that way until I met Johan. It began with my reactions to what *he* said. Once, for instance, when I walked with him in a culvert and we passed a flashing light, he said: "It's irritating when lamps blink like that." Then I knew immediately that he thought it was difficult to feel the truth only in glimpses and not continuously. And once, when I helped him with a crossword, and he happened to drop the pen, he said: "I get so upset that I drop the pen!" He revealed the truth without being aware of it himself.

She: Mm.

I: And when I didn't meet him, there were others who gave me information about him, if I didn't get it through myself.

She: Through yourself?

I: Yes, by being open and defenceless, so that his feelings would be able to come inside me. That's why that in town happened, I believe.

She: Oh, yes?

I: Yes, I released all outer control to leave room for him.

She: …

I: If I don't set myself aside and exterminate all reservations, I'll never be able to be really honest. But it's difficult to make yourself totally empty and receptive. To not see, but only hear and feel, as I did before I came to Ulleråker, makes it easier, but how do you exterminate all rational objections that pop up?

She: What do you mean by not seeing? Do you mean that you closed your eyes?

I: Yes, from the moment I fell on the bridge until I came to Ulleråker, I didn't open my eyes once. It felt forbidden. I didn't get to see the ambulance inside, and I didn't get to see the ambulance guy who sat beside me at the stretcher. At the emergency department my eyes were closed too.

She: But I still don't understand why you're doing it.

I: Because I want to know what Johan feels, so that I can be open to him and not be frightened of his innermost.

She: …

I: I deceived them, but I had to let it continue until it ended by itself.

She: Yeah?

I: Yes, when I lay there on the bridge, I thought that if Johan had come and asked me to rise and go away from there, I would have been able to do that, because it would have meant that he was ready to take responsibility for it himself. But I knew that he would only had placed himself among the other observers and pretended not to know me, if he had been there.

She: What did you think before you collapsed, then?

I: At first, I thought it was strange that I couldn't walk, and thought that I had to try to get away from there, but then I accepted it and disconnected my sanity and let my body prevail. I would never get to know what it meant otherwise, I thought.

She: And did you get to know it?

I: No, but I know that it had something to do with Johan. He is so little and helpless...

She: ...

I: When I stood there on the bridge a drunk guy came up to me and said: Hey, brother!

She: Yes?

I: Yes, as if he felt that I were...

She: But why should you identify with Johan, do you mean?

I: Because I recognize myself in him and can't resist his subconscious call for help. He is the way I was when I was a teenager.

She: Yes, but why must that imply that you take over his feelings?

I: I don't know.

She: What kind of emotions is it, then?

I: All that he isn't able to feel and bear consciously.

She: Such as…?

I: Fear, helplessness, pain, sorrow, confusion, sexual arousal, love…

She: But how can you know that it's his feelings and not your own?

I: Because I don't find any explanation for it, no matter how much I immerse myself in it. At last I'm forced to question it, and then my own feeling or reaction usually comes up instead, so that I can dismiss his, and separate myself from him at just that point. I believe that he gets it back then, but acknowledged and less frightening, since it hasn't scared me.

She: But how do you mean that it happens, when you never meet?

I: He's affected by my letters. If I didn't write to him, it probably wouldn't work. It's the letters that keep it alive.

She: What do *you* get out of doing it, then?

I: I don't know. Nothing… To be honest, it's very exhausting to be invaded by alien and incomprehensible feelings all the time! I'm almost not able to cope with it.

She: No, but there must be a reason for this happening, and that's what I want to come to.

I: Yes, that I want to help him because I love him.

She: But he doesn't love you?

I: No, not consciously.

She: But doesn't that feel wrong to you? That it isn't mutual, I mean.

I: No, the important thing isn't to get, but to give. Or as it says in the Bible: Love does not seek its own. It bears everything, believes everything, endures everything… But sometimes I wonder how much is needed… He would perhaps rather let me die than he…

She: What?

I: When I lay in the ambulance and my head rolled aside, the ambulance guy took my wrist and searched for the pulse. He perhaps thought I had died.

She: Mm.

I: I become sad when I think of it.

She: Why is that?

I: Because he didn't have to… I didn't mean to scare him. But I didn't know that he observed me so carefully.

She: Well, they always do, you know, if something would…

I: Yes, but I thought that he didn't care whether I lived or died.

She: You didn't?

I: No, I hadn't expected that. And the guy in the other ambulance, put his hand on my head, so it felt as if he… confirmed me.

She: Did you travel in *two* ambulances?

I: Yes, first in one to Ackis, and then in another to Ulleråker. I misused society's resources.

She: Well, you can't…

I: Yes, I know that I deceived and used them. But I couldn't help it. In the emergency room there was a nurse who became angry with me and asked me to stop fooling around.

She: Really?

I: Yes, I wonder if she usually says like that to people who come in with a broken leg also?

She: Hardly.

I: No, and if you work in health care, you shouldn't have prejudices about certain diseases, I think.

She: No, you wouldn't think so.

I: But never mind.

She: Well, I wonder if… Have you told your parents that you have been at Ulleråker?

I: No, I haven't, and I won't do it, either.

She: No, just what I thought.

I: But Lasse's parents know about it.

She: They do?

I: Yes, Lasse has told them. But they haven't said anything about it to me.

She: At your job then, what do they say there?

I: Nothing. I don't think that they know about it. I was on vacation when it happened, and I didn't report myself sick.

She: Didn't the hospital do that?

I: I don't know. It's possible that my boss knows about it. But she hasn't said anything, either.

…

I: If I could only understand what it meant…

She: Yes, but don't you think it was an expression for something from your childhood then?

I: No, it doesn't feel that way. And I know that it has to do with Johan.

She: But maybe you project your own problems on him?

I: No, why should I? I really want to feel everything I need to. I'm not afraid of it. But what I am doing for Johan now, I would have done for my own sake when I was a teenager. I wanted to open myself to the subconscious and find out what should happen. But I didn't dare release control and risk winding up in a mental hospital without knowing if they would be able to help me. I wouldn't dare do it now either, if it were about myself. They don't use primal therapy in Swedish hospitals, and medicines and common psychotherapy don't cure anybody. You have to manage on your own. But Johan doesn't know how to do it, and therefore I must help him. The problem is, that I myself don't know enough, either.

Hyperventilation, a presenting condition with people who have a nervous tendency of breathing over their normal need. They experience not getting enough air, which they try to compensate for by deep breathing. The forced breathing leads to a powerful removal of carbon dioxide from the blood. In connection with this, there is a tendency for change in the blood fluid's composition, which causes increased muscle excitability. With extreme h. cramps occur in the hands and feet, so called hyperventilation tetany as well as dizziness. H. is often combined with other nervous symptoms such as a lump sense in the throat, "globus hystericus", difficulty swallowing, and a tendency to gasp and rasp. H. is considered an anxiety phenomenon for therefore predisposed people. (Medical Reference Book)

Eva-Lena still doesn't have any explanation for her physical attack – which accordingly was psychically caused and led to her winding up at Ulleråker – but she maintains that it was about Johan. When we talked, I suggested that it perhaps rather was caused by something in her childhood, and reminded her of Janov's theories, which among other things involve that you act out denied feelings as long as you haven't experienced them.

But she didn't go along with that. Everything strange that happens to her, is originating in Johan's problems, she claims, and she's not open to other and more plausible explanations.

I have been at Ulleråker. There was no point in it, but I don't regret letting it happen.

I don't know the point in trying to help Johan. This, that I do, which he doesn't know about, can't affect him. Or can it? I don't know. I may just imagine everything. Lasse is perhaps right when he says that I'm crazy. I'm a crazy, middle aged hag with hanging tits who hunts for young boys, he says. Once, when we were fighting, and Johan defended himself with a knife, he said: "They should never have let you out of the madhouse!"

But it wasn't because I believed that Johan should get help, that I went to Ulleråker. I just wanted to find out how much they would understand. I know I must get through it myself. But what if I can't manage? And I don't know what's wrong. I don't know what it is, and I don't know how to sort it out.

I think I identify with Johan to learn to understand him so that I shall be able to help him when he is ready to help himself. That's why I'm not quite myself sometimes. I'm mixed with him, and I must continue to be, until I have taken a stand to, and sorted out everything that doesn't fit into my mind and body.

Kicki believes that I chose this explanation to avoid dealing with my own problems. Instead of investing in myself, I devote myself to him, she believes. If that's true, I still can't do anything about it, because I can't just ignore him and turn my back on him and walk away from him. And I can't separate us as long as I don't know what belongs to him and what belongs to me.

Eva-Lena called and talked about Lasse. He evidently can't accept that she doesn't want to lay him and continues to try to force himself on her with violence.

Earlier he also has tried to put different things in her, she said. First, I didn't understand. "Things?" I said. "What kind of things?" Well, there were cucumbers and bananas and bottles or anything whatever with the right shape. I find it so hard to understand that she has let him do it. I would never go along with anything like that!

And you can wonder what drove him to do it. I think it seems so awful. At the same time as he, for example, pressed a cucumber into her, he could say something like: "Now you're going to get a real fucking nigger cock! Is it pleasurable? Is it big enough, or would you like me to fetch something thicker?"

I almost can't believe it's true.

Sometimes it feels so meaningless to write to Johan. Why do I keep on doing it? What is it I hope for? That he will start assisting? But he doesn't even answer my letters. He doesn't do anything at all. Why do I accept that? I don't understand why I'm so compliant. I can't assert myself against him. As soon as I try, I'm forced to back off again.

But it isn't his fault that he can't manage it, and I can't leave him. Thought sometimes I'm angry and wish I could force him to answer. I think there must be *something* he could write or do. Once I sent him a letter with questions about what he likes to eat and things like that. Because I want to know everything about him. What kind of food he likes, how many girls he has laid, if he is for or against nuclear energy, what kind of books he likes to read, if he has heard of primal therapy, and all that kind of things.

But he didn't answer me then, either. I don't require him to be able to do the impossible, but I don't understand why he doesn't do anything *at all*.

To make an apt answer is a joy to a man, and a word in season, how good it is! (Proverbs 15:23)

Papa called and wanted me to come over. I was busy with washing the dishes, and first we talked a little, but then he asked if I could come. Well, I thought, I'll finish this first, and then I'll go.

But I didn't manage to finish washing before he called again and wondered if I wouldn't come soon. "Aren't you coming?*" "Yes, certainly," I said. "I didn't know there was such a hurry! I was washing, and I thought I would finish first." "Yes, but take a taxi, I'll pay." At first, I didn't think it was so acute, but more as if he felt lonely and a little down and wanted to talk, but then it seemed so very urgent suddenly. He sounded a little odd, I thought. "Yes, certainly, I'm coming," I said and got dressed and called a taxi and went away immediately.*

When I sat in the car, I felt very uneasy. My God, he's not going to kill himself, is he? I thought. But when I got there and rang the doorbell, he came and opened. He slammed the door open and began to yell fiercely at me. He lost control of his mouth and went on continuously: "What the hell do you mean, here I lend you my car, and then it isn't washed underneath *when I get it back!"*

I was taken aback and felt completely put out. I tried to say something, but I was so sorry that I started to cry, and I didn't get out a comprehensible word. I didn't scold him back, and I didn't ask him what kind of a fucking lunatic he was that behaved like he did – I just stood there and took it.

Finally, he calmed down, and I went in and sat down and talked with him. But I didn't say anything about his behaviour. I never have. Afterwards I thought: Why on earth didn't I get mad at him?

Because I've never been *angry. What do women do, who cannot be angry? Well, they* cry*. And that's what I have done. I cried when I was little, when I should have been angry with papa because he was so unjust and did things that I didn't want him to do, and I cry now. But preferably I would of course be able to object and defend myself.*

I: What are we going to do now? What would you like to do, Kicki? I already know what Lasse wants, but what would you like to do?

Kicki: Don't drink more now.

I: You perhaps want the same? After all, you have

always been interested in him.

She: Yes, but stop now.

I: And he in you. He's always wanted to lay you.

Lasse: Stop it!

I: But you have told me so! And now you have the opportunity!

He: …

I: And he's a devil of a fucker, so you don't need to worry that it won't be successful. He can get a hard on under any circumstances and carry on forever. "Now you'll get it, so that you can't sit for three days!" as he usually says.

Lasse: Stop it now, damn it!

I: Another variant is like this: "Now you'll get it, so that you burst!" Doesn't that sound wonderful? He's really a tough guy in bed, Lasse!

She: Now I'm leaving.

I: Leaving? No, now is when the fun begins. Isn't it Lasse? We don't want her to leave, do we?

He: No, stay.

I: Yes, listen to him! He doesn't want you to go. Now we'll take our clothes off and get started instead.

He: Yes, some group sex would be fine!

She: I don't get why you're carrying on like this, Eva-Lena.

I: You don't? Well, it's to help you two to finally get to do it. Start taking off your clothes now!

He: Yes, do that.

I: You too. Take off your shirt and pants. You must

set an example here, you know! And now you, Kicki.

She: No, I'm going to leave.

I: But you're the one who usually says that one must dare to show oneself naked in mind and body. Prove that you stand up for that now!

She: No, this time I prefer to keep my clothes on.

I: Really? What's so special about this time, then?

She: Well, you're drunk, for example!

I: So, you don't want to fuck Lasse? But then he will be disappointed. Won't you, Lasse?

He: Yes, maybe…

I: Yes, listen to him! He wants to do it with you. It wouldn't surprise me if he already has a hard on. May I feel if you have a hard on?

He: Hands off, damn it!

I: Yes, he has one! He's already horny. Should I take it out, so that you'll see what you'll miss in case you don't take your clothes off and lie down?

He: Stop it!

I: Show your cock to mom now, and don't be shy! No, what do I say? To Kicki, I mean.

She: Goodbye!

I: Look! She's leaving now! Are you going to just sit there and let her go now, when the goal is so close?

He: Don't care about her fucking crap! Come back and take off your clothes instead, and then all three of us can go to bed.

I: Yes, come and take off your clothes, so that Lasse can realize his big dream!

She: No thanks.

I: Do you want to watch while he and I fuck, then? He won't mind. He knows that I don't want to lay him, and that I'm interested in another, but that doesn't matter to him. The main thing is that he gets to fuck. And I can pretend that he is Johan.

She: Stop it now, Eva-Lena! This isn't funny!

I: No, it isn't. It isn't funny being married to a sex machine who doesn't give a shit about who you are and only sees a hole that he can empty himself into. Do you know what he used to say at the time when I still went along with laying him? "Your cunt is like a slop bucket," he used to say. And then he emptied his slop in it.

He: Shut up now!

I: Why? If she's going to fuck you, it's only fair that she gets to know which style you make use of!

She: I'm going now, Eva-Lena.

I: No, look what a hard on he has! Won't you stay and let him screw you after all?

She: Goodbye!

I: Well, in that case he'll have to be satisfied with me. Come on then! Let's fuck!

She: Goodbye, I said!

He: Bye-bye. And pay no attention to her!

…

He: Now, you fucking slut, you're finished with your little game!

I: Yes, now I'll get it so that I burst, won't I?

Last Saturday I was with Eva-Lena. She had started drinking even before I came, and if I had been really tough, I would have turned at the doorstep as soon as I realized that she was drunk.

But I wasn't that tough. Lasse was also at home, and all three of us sat and talked, while Eva-Lena kept on drinking. She was very provocative to both him and me, and in the end she went completely off the rails, which made me finally get started and leave. But I shouldn't have sat there at all and listened to her! I should have objected at an early point, to both her and Lasse.

Because I didn't get any support from him. In the beginning, I actually believed that he and I had the same attitude to what she was carrying on with, but then it turned out that it wasn't that way at all, and that should of course have made me get up and leave immediately.

And I didn't stay much longer, but it was as if I had difficulty grasping that he wasn't distancing himself from Eva-Lena's behaviour in the same way as I was. On the contrary, it turned out that he was using it for his own dubious purposes, and that was very hard for me to comprehend.

I: Eva-Lena.

Johan: Hello, Eva-Lena! Do you hear who this is?

I: No?

He: It's me, Johan. You weren't asleep, were you?

I: No, I was reading.

He: Reading? Wow!

I: …

He: Can you please stop now?

I: Stop what?

He: Writing letters. I can't take this any longer. I'm completely cracked by this. I don't understand the letters, and I think they are unpleasant.

I: …

He: So, would you please stop now?

I: No, I can't.

He: If you don't stop I'll report you to the police!

I: Yes, you can do that if you think it helps!

He: But I don't feel well by never being left alone! I become nervous and get stomach aches.

I: You can throw the letters away, unread.

He: Yes, that's exactly what I do. I have stopped reading them and throw away all I receive, unopened.

I: The old ones, then, what have you done with them?

He: I have thrown them away too. They were unpleasant and sick and nothing to save.

I: …

He: So, you'll be wasting your money by continuing.

I: …

He: Are you still there?

I: Yes. What's wrong with your stomach, then?

He: I'm on the sick-list with gastric catarrh.

I: In that case, it's no good idea to drink, I think.

He: To drink?

I: Yes, to drink alcohol, as you have obviously done now?

He: No, it's no problem…

I: …

He: So, can you please stop now? I can't cope with all your letters with strange content.

I: …

He: Like in this last one… Now, damned it, she's begun to send rolled up banknotes as well! I thought. But I don't need any screw drivers. My tool-box is full. It wasn't good, either. But I understand that there is something you want to get rid of.

I: Yes.

…

He: Well, that's all I wanted to say. Bye-bye!

I: This is so unfair! You just escape and leave me alone with all this shit.

He: Escape?

I: Yes, but I'm the one who's right, so I don't have anything to be sad about.

He: I perhaps shouldn't have called…

I: Yes, I think it was good that you did.

He: …

I: Everything is your pop's fault!

He: Don't drag my poor parents into this again, because then I get upset!

I: But it's their fault that…

He: There isn't anything wrong with my parents! I always, for example, ask my mother for advice before I do something important.

I: How about your pop then?

He: No, with him it's worse… I become so fucking pissed at him sometimes. Once I went after him with a knife.

I: Why did you do that?

He: Because he didn't like the girl I brought home.

I: What did he do when you went after him, then? Hide in the wardrobe?

He: No, he locked himself into another room. But he was right. She was a fucking whore who didn't fit into our home.

I: Your pop is a captain, isn't he?

He: No, not any longer. He has risen in degrees so quickly that he soon believes that he is God himself.

I: Yes, there you see yourself that…

He: But I love my parents highly and purely!

I: Yes, but that's what's wrong. Because they don't love you highly and purely back.

He: Yes, you bet they do!

I: No, because in that case you wouldn't smoke and drink and be unhappy.

He: But that's what *you* do?

I: Yes, but I know that nobody wants me, so I don't let myself be fooled.

He: …

I: Are you still there?

He: Yes, I'm thinking.

I: About what?

He: You have been in mental hospital, haven't you?

I: Why do you ask?

He: Because someone said so.

I: Who?

He: Lasse.

I: *Lasse*? When did you talk to him?

He: Last summer. He called me and asked for you. He didn't know where you were and had got the idea that you were here.

I: I see.

He: Then he called again and told me that he had found out where you were.

I: …

He: He said that you were at the funny farm.

I: I see.

He: Were you?

I: Yes.

…

He: There is something I would like to ask you.

I: Yes?

He: Did you tell anything about me then?

I: When?

He: When you were… an inpatient.

I: Locked up.

He: Yes, locked up. Did you say anything about me then?

I: Only that you were a work-mate. I didn't mention any names, but I told them that you existed.

He: That I existed?

I: Yes, that I had met you.

…

He: What did I do that made you start writing all those letters to me?

I: It wasn't anything you did.

He: Well, there must have been. Something I did or didn't do.

I: Didn't do, then.

He: And what was it that I *didn't* do?

I: Admitted how it was.

He: How it was with what?

I: …

He: You have to explain it a little more in detail.

I: …

He: Do you mean that we belong together like yin and yang?

I: Yes.

He: But damn it, Eva-Lena! Don't say that to me. It's impossible.

I: No, because I know that you exist.

He: You can't know that.

I: Yes, I do.

He: But when you reach your hand out, I'm not there.

I: No, but I know it anyway.

…

He: Are you still there?
I: Yes.
He: Can you promise to stop writing, then?
I: Yes, there is probably nothing more to say…
He: There isn't?
I: No, what should that be?
He: Well, I don't know…
I: …
He: You promise to lay off, then?
I: Sure.
He: So now there is nothing left?
I: I suppose so.
He: Well, I hope it's true, because I can't cope with having it like this any longer. Don't you realize how fucking sick it is?
I: What do you mean?
He: What you do.
I: But I…
He: Listen to me now! I'm *afraid* of you. I don't want anything to *do* with you. You're *sick*.
I: Yes, I have been locked up at the funny farm.
He: That isn't what I meant…
I: …
He: You're too old for me.
I: Yes, you're just a little boy.
He: I feel sorry for you, but I don't like you.
I: …
He: It's so fucking annoying.
I: What is?

He: Everything. *You* are annoying.

I: In what way?

He: Well, you offer yourself like a… Are you lost to all sense of shame?

I: No.

…

He: Do you promise that you'll release me now?

I: …

He: Are we in agreement about that?

I: Yes, I suppose so…

He: Suppose?

I: Yes.

…

He: Best wishes.

I: Thanks. The same to you.

He: Live a good life.

I: Sure. You too.

He: Yes, you can fix it. Everything will turn out well.

I: …

He: Bye-bye.

I: Bye.

When the moose went down to the lake to drink he saw his reflection in the water's surface and said loudly to himself:

"I'm the king of the forest, I'm the king of the forest!"

Then the bear, who had heard him, came out of the woods and asked him in a threatening voice:

"What did you say?"

Whereupon the moose turned his head, grinned apologetically and said:

"Oh, I always talk too much when drinking!"

Anita and I have been to Baldakinen and danced. It was nice, because it was long since the last time, and I got to dance a lot.

Baldis is the place where I met Leif, about half a year after it ended with Bosse. We danced many dances during the evening, and then he went home with me. We drank tea and talked. And as we were sitting there on the sofa, he suddenly threw himself over me. At first, I defended myself a little, but then I thought: Yes, we can as well hop in bed, so that we can continue to talk when we have got this over with!

And that's what we did. And he became sweaty, so it began to drop on me, and he got an orgasm almost at once.

Later I tried to find out why he was so tense. I asked him about his childhood and his parents, and he said that he had had a delightful upbringing, completely without problems. But I didn't believe that, because why did he have such difficulties with the physical part in that case? His parents were religious, and they might have had taboos about sexuality, I thought and proposed. But he didn't want to agree with that. No, everything had been so good!

Though that tension with him never passed over. It was modified a little, but it never disappeared during the half year that we were together.

In the mental area we weren't especially alike, either. While I wanted to discuss all problems, and try to find out the reasons behind them, he preferred to stick his head in the sand and be silent. I finally began to feel that we couldn't continue as we did. It didn't give anything. We couldn't talk properly, and our physical life together was not satisfying. So, I started to go out a little, and one evening I met Peter, which lead to that I finally ended it with Leif.

Unknown guy: Take a seat while you wait, and I'll soon be with you. What would you like to drink? I can offer coffee or a grog.

I: A grog then. Though I have already drunk several of them.

He: Really?

I: Yes, I'm already drunk. Didn't you notice, when you came up to me? Because that's why you asked me to come along, wasn't it?"

He: What do you want then?

I: Anything.

He: Rum and cola?

I: Yes, that would be fine.

…

I: Cheers!

He: Cheers.

I: Do you live here alone?

He: Yes.

I: …

He: How quiet you are.

I: Yes, I can't come up with anything to say. It's completely empty!

He: …

I: Do you often take girls with you like this?

He: No. Do you often accompany guys like this?

I: Yes.

He: …

I: Do you have any music?

He: Certainly. What do you want to hear?

I: Elvis. Do you have Elvis?

He: Yes.

I: Put Elvis on then.

He: …

I: Do you like Elvis?

He: Yes, quite a lot.

I: This one is good! (start to sing) "You ain't nothing but a hound dog, crackin' all the time…" (stop singing) This one they often played in the *raggarbilar*.

He: What?

I: I was a *raggarbrud* when I was younger.

He: I see.

I: What were you when you were younger?

He: Nothing special.

I: What are you now, then?

He: What?
I: What's your job?
He: I'm self-employed.
I: In what business?
He: Plumbing.
…
I: Now it's your turn to talk.
He: …
I: Say something, to show that you're alive!
He: …
I: What a dilemma, isn't it?
He: What?
I: Dilemma! Don't you know what dilemma means? First, we have "di", then we have "lem" and then we have "ma", which here is a shortened form of mamma.
He: …
I: If you think I behave weird, it's because I'm on the run from the funny farm.
He: Don't be silly.
I: But it's true! I've been locked up since the thirty-first of July.
He: …
I: Now I'm getting tired.
He: Come on then, and let's go to bed.
I: Mm… "If she isn't good enough for anything else, she's at least good enough to be a candlestick, said the devil, turned the witch up and down."
He: What?
I: …

He: Come on now.

I: No, now I'm going to tell you what it's like to be locked up at the funny farm. (start to sing) "Now I'm going to tell you about a little worm, and the worm is called Maaax!" (stop singing) To be locked up at the funny farm is fucking pleasant, if you can't manage to save your face any longer. The worm Max will soon pop off! No, the dachshund Max will soon pop off. It's difficult to say. Try it yourself and you'll see. Dachshund Max... Don't you want to? Don't you think it's fun with wordplays? No, then I won't insist. Where was I now? Yes, at the funny farm. Have you been locked up there sometime?

He: No.

I: But I have. I have been there for psychi... psychri... psychriatric care. No, is it really called that? It sounds so strange, I think. But that's what I have been there for.

He: Come on, let's go to bed now.

I: (start to sing) "Now I'm going to tell you about..." (stop singing).

He: Come on.

I: No, I'm obviously not...

He: ...

I: Where are you? What are you doing?

He: ...

I: Oh, I'm really drunk... What are you doing back there? Do you have a *bed* here?

He: Yes, come and lie down.

I: Have you undressed?

He: Yes, you do it too.

I: No, you may do it.

He: Come here, then.

I: And then we'll fuck, won't we?

He: Yes. Give me a hand here.

I: No, I'm going now.

He: What?

I: I'm going now.

He: Why?

I: I'm going now.

He: Why now?

I: Because I must stop.

He: What?

I: I must stop believing too much about people. You only loose, doing that.

He: …

I: If you trust people who aren't able to feel the truth, you will be fooled.

He: Come now and stop fooling around.

I: No, I'm leaving.

He: Suck then. Come and suck!

I: No, I want all of you. It's not just your cock I want. Purely in principle, that is.

He: …

I: By the way, do you know why the Norwegians stick their cocks into the water?

He: No.

I: Because they've heard that the sea sucks.

He: …

I: Funny, isn't it?

…

He: Can you jack me off, then?

I: No, you can do it yourself.

He: But it's more pleasant when you do it.

I: Not for me.

He: But I can do it pleasant for you, too.

I: No, now I have to go. Bye-bye black bird and have a good time.

I don't understand why Eva-Lena must carry on as she does. First, she goes to Solan and lets herself be offered booze, and then she goes to town and hopes that somebody will come and make contact with her. One of these days – or nights, *rather – she will meet someone who doesn't tolerate her false pretences and provocative behaviour, and then you never know what can happen. She could be beaten or even killed.*

But she doesn't seem to care about it. She probably believes that there is no risk. But to judge by what she has told me about how it can happen, I think she is asking for trouble by acting the way she does.

I: Leave me alone! I'm washing the dishes.

Lasse: Yes, I know that. But now I want to fuck you in the ass!

I: Why?

He: Because it would be pleasurable. Tight and pleasurable.

I: Not for me.

He: Yes, it will.

I: But I'm a guy.

He: It doesn't matter.

I: I'm tall and slender and have light hair and glasses.

He: Pull down your trousers and lean over the sink.

I: So, it's a guy you want?

He: No, you're the one I want to fuck in the ass.

I: Why have you never wanted it before, then?

He: Stop bitching and pull down your pants!

I: But it will be painful.

He: No way. I'll fetch some Vaseline and grease you up.

I: And I don't understand why you want to do it.

He: To make you realize a thing about yourself that you may find useful.

I: What kind of thing?

"How do you trot now, Brunte?" asked the farmer, rode backwards. (Saying)

When I had gone to bed and fallen asleep Johan called. Lasse was out to fill the car or something, so I didn't need to worry about that he would hear what I said.

Johan had been to Baldis and had just come home. I asked him if he hadn't met any girl, since he had gone home alone.

"No, I was pleasant, and I was spiritual, and I danced well, but nothing helped," he said.

I don't want him to call me only when he is drunk and maybe randy and hasn't gotten anyone else. I asked why he never calls when he is sober.

"Because I'm afraid of you," he said.

I don't remember everything we said. Towards the end he told me that he was freezing.

"Put on a blanket then," I said.

"I already have a blanket, but it doesn't help. I may call the dog."

"Yes, at least it warms a bit, said the girl, peed in her stockings," I said.

When he laughed I felt glad. I love you, I thought. I love him, but I don't know what to do to help him become free.

Afterwards I felt pleased. This time he didn't call me to try to convince me to stop writing letters to him, and he wasn't angry.

But now I feel sad. Why couldn't his mother have loved him, so he could have avoided being unhappy? As soon as he was born she abandoned him. I love him, but what he didn't got from her, no one else can give him now. If you don't get what you need at the right time, and from the right person, it becomes too late. The only thing you can do later, is to feel the need and experience the pain of not having had it satisfied.

You must stop hoping for everything that was hope-less, if you shall be free. When you smoke and drink you can't feel. You can't feel hopelessness as long as you give yourself consolation. That's why I shall stop smoking and drinking soon. As soon as I manage to leave Johan alone with it, and manage to be alone myself, I shall quit.

Again, if two lie together, they are warm; but how can one be warm alone? (Ecclesiastes 4:11)

Lasse called and asked if he could come over for a while. I know that he doesn't have anyone to talk with about his problem – Eva-Lena he can't turn to, because she is the one who is his problem – so I let him come.

Then he sat here on my sofa and complained that she runs out at nights and comes home affected by booze. He thinks it's so tough that he can't trust her and doesn't know what she is up to – and you can understand that.

When he had gotten the worst out, I put in a little carefully that it would perhaps be just as well with a divorce – I know that Eva-Lena wants that – and then he admitted that he has begun to realize that a separation might be the only solution. But he doesn't think that Eva-Lena is ready for it yet. She couldn't handle living alone as she is right now, he thinks. And that's maybe true in a way, because if she could really do what she claims that she wants to do, she would apply for a divorce and move away from him right away instead of keep waiting for them to agree about it.

On Sunday I went to the movies. Afterwards a guy in a Volvo gave me a lift home. It has happened before when I've walked in town, that guys have stopped and offered me a ride. I don't know why.

Well, I do know why. And I know why I ride along. They come instead of Johan and do what I want *him* to do. They try to take his place without knowing it themselves. That's why I don't say no when they ask. It's to Johan I say yes. But in the end, there is no way to look away from reality, and I have to say no.

He stopped on Ågatan and asked if I had got a light. It's on Ågatan the *raggare* carry on these days. When I was young it was on Svartbäcksgatan, before it became a pedestrian street.

But this one wasn't a *raggare*. He asked if I were in a hurry, or if I wanted to go with him to his home and share a bottle of wine. And I wanted to, rather than go home to Lasse, but I couldn't, because he wasn't Johan, and Johan is the only one I want. He is the one I want to meet and drink wine with and open myself for. I can't do it with anyone else.

Eva-Lena has been out again and gone along in a car. I don't understand what she is carrying on with! Is she trying to relive the time when we were young and went to Svartbäcksgatan and let ourselves be picked up by unknown guys, or what is she doing?

That was when, and where, she started to drink. If she hadn't met Lasse – or if he hadn't come back to her, rather – you don't know how it could have ended. If she hadn't killed herself, she could very well have become an alcoholic.

And it's still not too late. I think she seems to be in a fair way to go there now instead. Without Lasse she obviously can't resist drinking. But this time it's she who is leaving him and not the opposite.

Before I met Johan, I believed that Lasse loved me, but now I have realized that he doesn't. I haven't loved him, either. He shouldn't have come back, when it was over between us for a while in the beginning, and he shouldn't have married me.

Last night I dreamed that Johan and I would move in together and get married. We had already gotten an apartment, and when we came there, he gave me a ring. I gave him another ring, and when he put it on he said: "Something like this I have always wanted."

When we had been in the apartment for a while, Lasse turned up. I didn't want to let him in, because I had a feeling that he would try to destroy us. I pushed him out in the staircase and screamed: "Go away from here you fucking homo!"

I think he is homosexual, though he doesn't realize it himself. Partly, anyway. I believe that he perceives Johan in me and gets turned on by him.

Lasse came by for a while, and when we talked, he told me about his mother, whom he obviously has been very disappointed in. According to Eva-Lena, he has never talked with her about such things. To her he has on the contrary asserted that he doesn't think that the past is anything to poke into. So that he talks with me about it, I should probably take as a complement.

But there was some kissing and hugging also, by his initiative. I didn't really know how I should react to it. I had nothing against it, but I didn't think it felt especially motivated. After all, he comes here because he needs to talk.

When Johan wants to get a girl, he goes to Baldakinen and dances. I don't know how it is there, because I have never been there. But Kicki goes there sometimes, so she may have met him occasionally without knowing it.

All the girls he dances with and maybe goes along with afterwards... They get to see him and talk with him and touch him... Why can't I get to do that?

I want to meet him and make love to him. Sometimes I think that I should also go to Baldakinen and get a chance to see him. But I cannot even dance, and he would probably just pretend that he didn't know me, if he caught sight of me there.

And I don't dare to go home to him. I scarcely dare to call. I don't know how many times I have tried and then just have been silent on the phone until he has hung up again. I cannot resit calling, though I know that I won't be able to talk. It feels like it should be he, and not I, who starts the conversation.

I believe that it is his true self in me who calls and wants him to confirm it. If it were me, I would be able to talk with him as I do when he calls *me*. It is his false self who doesn't want to meet me and doesn't want me to write letters. It feels threatened by me, because I have seen through it and want it to disappear.

But his true self loves me. I know it, because why would I otherwise want to talk about everything with him? I would not be able to do that, if I didn't feel that he understood me. His true self accepts me no matter what I do. It accepts everything except for my false self, and my false self is much weaker than my true self, so there is nothing that can hinder me from receiving love.

Sometimes I think that he doesn't know himself that he loves me. There are maybe so many problems in the way that he can't feel it. But I know that he sees me and understands me and loves me. That's why I can't believe his false self when it claims that he won't have anything to do with me.

And if I have prophetic powers, and understand all mysteries and all knowledge, and if I have all faith, so as to remove mountains, but have not love, I am nothing. (1 Corinthians 13:2)

Lasse has been here again. Now it's more that he comes by so that he and I can see each other, and not because he has a great need to talk about his problem with Eva-Lena. I said that I think we should tell her that we meet, but he didn't agree with that. He wants for us to wait. I tried to say that I know that she wouldn't take offence, because she has encouraged us to try to find out what he and I have in common, but that wasn't what he was afraid of, he said. I actually never got to know why he wants us to keep it secret.

When we sat on the sofa and talked, he hugged me again, and I didn't push him away. I can't claim that I'm in love with him, and I can't say that I feel especially physically attracted to him, but he interests me as a person. He always has. Already from the very beginning, I noticed that we had certain similarities.

Especially one time I felt it very clearly. It was when I was together with Bosse, and we were out in the country all four of us, in mamma's and papa's summer cottage.

We had bought crayfish and booze and were going to have a crayfish party, because it was in August. And Eva-Lena drank to much, and Bosse drank too much, while Lasse and I shared that we always exercised moderation, so when Eva-Lena was out in the woods and crept under the spruces, and Bosse got a headache and went to bed, Lasse and I sat together out by the fire and talked. We met on the verbal plane, though there was possibly a physical attraction as well, but from my side there was never a question of it coming to expression.

Johan has got a secret phone number, so that I won't be able to call him anymore. But I *want to* be able to call him! I can't manage being rejected by him. I don't understand why I have to.

Though he receives my letters. And if it isn't possible to call him, I'll need to find the courage to go to his home instead. But then he will probably move and get a secret address as well.

I ran into Åke in town, and we stopped and talked for a while. He was the same as ever, and he still lived with his friend that he moved to when I asked him to pick up his things and disappear. – Then there was plain speaking! – But we weren't disagreed, because later we joined hands with packing and taking away all his things.

Åke I also met at Baldakinen. Who is it that has said that it's impossible to meet your intended at a dance restaurant?

The first evening there was nothing – no physical intercourse, I mean – but then it wasn't long before we ended up in bed. There was nothing strange about that, I thought and assumed, but he probably had needed more time, because he couldn't do it the first time we tried. And that locked him so much that he couldn't do it the second time, either. He didn't become shaky and sweaty as Leif, but he lost his erection. At first, he had a hard on, but when he was about to do it, he slacked.

Yes, and then I thought that I must help him with that. Once when he had just showered and walked around in only his boxers, I flew at him and seduced him directly, before he had time to think. It happened on the floor in the hallway. And then it went very well! So after that occurrence, the problem was over and done with once and for all.

On the mental plane I had to sink to his level, and there wasn't anything wrong with that level, other than it wasn't mine. And he was so locked. When it became difficult sometimes, he could sit in an armchair and be completely shut down. He crept together and shut down, and you could see that he felt like a little child. I tried both physically and psychically to loosen him up, and some things came out, such as that his mother had forced him under water when he was afraid to shower his hair, for example, and other, similar things.

But then I got tired of it, because it only happened two or three times that I came really close to him and felt that we could have been together. All other time we just devoted ourselves to an easy-going life together that was mostly based on our bodies.

I went to Johan with a letter. He became angry when he saw me and didn't let me in. I don't understand why I'm not allowed to get close to him, when he is allowed to get close to me. Shouldn't it be the same for both of us?

But it isn't. Either he treats me as his worst enemy or as if I don't exist. He can't confirm me, for then he must first confirm himself, and he isn't capable of that. It's only with himself he can confirm me, but he himself is dead and buried.

Once he said that I was caught in a transparent bubble and couldn't get out. But it's he, and not me, who is trapped and living death! Why can't I realize that he will never try to get himself out and start to live? Why do I continue to hope that he will begin to care about himself, so that I can love him in reality? I'm so stupid to believe that I can influence him! It's only he who has influenced *me*. I have *let* him do it. But he doesn't dare to be open to me. He is so afraid of being put out, that he must use violence, or the threat of violence, if I just appear. He doesn't want to. He doesn't dare. He isn't able to do what he ought to do.

But I know him. He is unhappy. He wants to come out. He prays on his bare knees that someone will come and help him. How can I leave him then?

I can't. I love him. I cannot listen to his false self who says that I should leave him alone. He doesn't want to be left alone. He wants help. I must try. I cannot abandon him. It makes no difference that he gives me the cold, because I don't need his confirmation of my existence.

And when he rejects me, it's actually himself he is rejecting. If it were really me, I wouldn't be so insistent. In that case, I wouldn't try to force myself on him. But I want him to want himself! I can't stand it, that he doesn't open himself to his innermost and confirm it.

I: Eva-Lena.

Johan: If you come home to me one more time I'll send the dog on you!

I: …

He: Or smash your face and break all the bones in your body.

I: …

He: Do you hear what I'm saying?

I: Yes, but why are you so angry? I just wanted to give you a letter.

He: I don't want you running here. My home is my

castle and there I want to be left in peace!

I: …

He: If you hadn't gone of your own free will, I would have thrown you down the stairs.

I: Well, you almost did anyway! You actually took a stranglehold on me, if you don't remember.

He: Yes, I was so fucking upset.

I: And then you pushed me, so I almost fell.

He: Yes, keep away from here, because next time I might be more successful, so you'll have to walk like a babbling idiot the rest of your life.

I: But I just came to hand over that letter!

He: And then you put the pieces in my letter slot! Did you think that I would sit down and try to puzzle them together again?

I: No, I didn't. Did you?

He: …

I: Why did you tear the letter apart?

He: Because I was so fucking pissed!

I: Why?

He: Because I can't stand this anymore! So, keep away from here in the future!

I: Otherwise, you'll call the police, won't you?

He: Yes, when I said that, you were really scared!

I: No, I wasn't.

He: But you went away?

I: Yes, what else could I have done? Stayed outside your door, waiting for you to open it again? But I did think about tearing down that I-guard-this-house-sign before I left, because I don't think it works to try to scare away burglars when there are other, invisible enemies you are afraid of.

He: You'll never be able to find out my telephone number anyway!

I: No, it's secret so that your enemies won't be able to call you.

...

He: Yes, that's all I wanted to say. If you come here one more time, I cannot take responsibility for the consequences!

I'll soon be back, said the old hag, rode on the windmill blade.

(Saying)

No, I'm just joking! Your home is your castle and there you want to be left in peace.

Lasse just brawls. If he doesn't try to force himself on me physically, he attacks me mentally. He can, for example, sit in the easy chair by the stereo and smoke while he plays one of his records.

I hate his records! He only plays them to provoke me. If that weren't the case, he would just put on his earphones when he listens. He does it to point out that I'm not free of him yet and have to stay, even though I don't want to. He plays to assert himself and to show his power over me.

But he doesn't *have* any power over me! It isn't *me* he has power over. Sometimes I hate him so much that I think I could kill him. Why can't he leave me alone? Why can't he disappear from here, so I get rid of him? Why can't he *die*?

I don't want to be married to him any longer. I don't want to live with him. And I won't, either, only I have become strong enough to demand a divorce. Only I am strong enough and *separated* enough to go.

But Lasse probably want Johan to stay. He is the one he wanted to have anal sex with, and it's him he is friendly with, and sits and talks with, when he is in a good mood. Me he is only angry with.

This is a hell of music, said the church mouse on Sunday morning.

(Saying)

Lasse and I have continued to meet. It isn't completely problem-free when it comes to the physical part, and I have tried to explain to him that we won't do more than what feels true for the moment, but he doesn't seem to get it. Or if he gets it, he can't in any case comply with it.

But I want it to feel right. As soon as it doesn't, we won't go any further, I mean. But he always exceeds that limit, and every time it happens he becomes very altered. First, everything feels all right, but then he suddenly acts like he must force barriers and looks so strange and strained in his face. And that I resist him then, he cannot really accept.

That reminds me of a guy who I met at Baldis once. He seemed to be nice, and it turned out that he was a doctor at the Academic Hospital. But that wasn't what made me interested in him – it was that I found it so easy to talk with him. Among other things, I presented my viewpoints of alcohol and told him why I had stopped with all alcoholic drinks – because I had done that by then – and he listened and agreed.

The next time we met, he came to my home – and when I opened the door he stood there with a bottle of wine in his hand! I had been open to him and believed that we were completely in agreement, but apparently he hadn't understood a thing! A total waste, in other words! How can you come to me with wine after all I have said? I thought. "That one you can take home with you again!" I told him. I would have preferred to just slam the door, but okay, you may come in, so that we can talk. *Later he became so nervous that he had to open the bottle and drink a little to calm himself down.*

With him the fact was also, as with Lasse, that the physical need was impending. It was more important than anything else and had to have its release. We had built up a mutual understanding before, but it didn't help, because he couldn't resist the internal pressure and was forced to give in to it. He threw himself quite lite-

rally over me there on the sofa. So, then it was thanks and goodbye to him!

Unknown guy: Hello there!
   I: Yes?
   He: Are you called Christina?
   I: No, I'm not.
   He: The fact is, that I had arranged a meeting here, with a girl who is called that.
   I: I see.
   He: But she didn't come.
   I: No?
   …
   He: Do you work here?
   I: Yes.
   He: Are you a nurse?
   I: No.
   …
   He: Are you on your way home?
   I: Yes.
   He: Hop in then, and I'll give you a lift.
   …
   I: So, Kicki didn't come?
   He: No.
   I: And then you took me instead?
   He: Yes.
   I: Do you often replace girls that easily?
   He: …

I: Turn right here.

He: Where do you live then?

I: In Gränby.

He: Then we'll go to Gränby.

I: …

He: What's your name if it isn't Christina?

I: Lena.

He: And I'm Lars-Åke.

I: …

He: How quiet it became.

I: Yes, that's because no one is saying anything.

He: Yes, probably, ha, ha!

I: …

He: Put your hand here.

I: What?

He: Put your hand here on the shift stick.

I: Why?

He: So you'll get to know how it feels.

I: That's nothing to feel.

He: Well, wait and see. First yours like this, and then mine on yours.

I: …

He: That wasn't so dangerous, was it?

I: No, but it's rather sweaty.

He: Yes, it usually is, ha, ha!

…

I: Why do you stop?

He: I thought we could stay and talk a little.

I: About what?

He: Anything.

I: But I must go home.

He: Yes, I'm giving you a lift home.

I: But first we'll talk a little?

He: Yes, I thought so.

I: Why are you acting like this then?

He: …

I: Leave off! You wanted to talk, you said.

He: Yes.

I: Fucking strange way you have of talking!

He: Spread your legs a little and let me touch.

I: Stop it, I said!

He: Open your legs.

I: I can walk from here, if you don't want to give me a lift.

He: Let go of the handle.

I: Stop it, then!

He: But you don't need to…

I: Yes, I do!

He: …

I: You're like my husband.

He: …

I: But I'm going to divorce him. I'm not going to be married to him any longer.

He: …

I: I'm going to *leave* him, exactly as I'm going to leave *you* now! I'm not going to wait any longer for you to understand, because you'll never get it, anyway. I'm just going to leave and never come back.

Yes, and now what? Lasse came by late last evening, and almost at once we ended up in bed. I have always thought that you should be naked in both mind and body when you make love, but when we were undressing, he kept his sweater on, and then I thought: He doesn't want to be naked! *Or he* couldn't, *I felt and understood. But he came inside me, and I couldn't stand it and threw him off.* No! *I felt and bumped him away from me.*

Then he rushed up and home. Rush, rush, on with his clothes, bam and away! It was a darting exit, so to say! But I don't regret what I did, because it didn't feel right, and I want it to do that. We'll see if I hear from him again, or if he was so offended by being rejected that he won't call anymore.

I don't really know why Johan is afraid of Lasse. It's perhaps because Lasse reminds him of his papa. I believe that his papa is like Lasse, that he can't tolerate fear and helplessness.

As soon as Lasse notices that I am at a disadvantage, he attacks me. It's Johan he comes at then, and I can only stand by and watch. I have no right to take over and defend him in his place. He must be able to defend himself. He must learn to do that. It's a good thing that he can say no to anal sex, because otherwise I would be forced to go along with it when Lasse wants it.

171

If Johan were homosexual, or couldn't reject sexual invitations from men, he would be the one the other guy wanted to screw. Boys who have had a seductive mother and an authoritarian father must often play that role in a homosexual relationship. They must watch out for women and submit to men. That's why I thought I wasn't afraid of him the first time I met him. We stand on the same side against those like his pop and Lasse, who could rape both him and me.

At Ulleråker there was a guy that I think was homosexual. One evening, when the others had gone to bed, we sat in the day room and acted as if we had a party. We got drunk on imaginary vodka and juice. That he was homosexual – or at least bisexual – I suspected among other things because I got a card from him where he had written: "Eva-Lena! Live a pure life without any backbiting!"

Follow suit, dodderer, said the boy, played cards with his father.

(Saying)

I come to think about how it was when I told Bosse that it was Stig, my brother-in-law, who took my virginity. When he got to know it, he became so upset that he drew away and almost disappeared. I told him about it almost like a funny story – no, not a funny story, but I wasn't at all ashamed of it – and then he became very silent and strange. It might have been better if I had kept it to my-self, I thought afterwards. But I took for granted that he would look at it about the same way as I did and not take it so seriously.

The next evening, when he came to fetch me, I noticed from him that it still wasn't quite well. I asked what it was – though I almost understood – and then he said that he had considered if we perhaps shouldn't be together anymore. I had not expected him to say that, and I didn't understand why the thing with Stig had to change any-thing.

Then I thought that it surely would work out if I only got to talk with him. I have always been like that, that I believe that everything can be fixed! But he said: "If it has happened once, it can happen again." He didn't mean exactly with Stig, but he didn't trust me any-more, I felt. I tried to explain and pointed out that it had happened before I met him, and that it didn't have anything to do with us, but he was still very doubtful.

And I could understand that it felt strange to him, be-cause there he had gone around and felt responsibility for me and taken care of me, because I was so much younger than he was and still went to school and so on, and then it turned out that I wasn't at all as innocent as he had believed.

But finally, I managed to convince him that there was no reason for him to break up. I said that I understood that his confidence in me was wrecked, but that things

*that had happened before we met didn't have any impor-
tance for us, and then it felt like he could accept it, and
we reconciled and continued together.*

Unknown guy: You're not falling asleep, are you?
  I: No.
  He: What are you thinking of?
  I: Nothing special.
  He: You're not feeling sick, are you?
  I: No.
  …
  He: Have you drunk much this evening?
  I: I don't know. I was with a friend and we drank
there.
  He: I see.
  I: She showed me the outer parts of her labia.
  He: What did you say?
  I: She showed me the outer parts of her labia. But it
was actually *him* she showed them to.
  He: Who?
  I: I don't think she would have shown them to me.
  He: …
  I: She had a swelling there, that she wanted him to
look at.
  He: On her labia?
  I: Yes, on one of the outer parts.
  He: And she showed it to you?
  I: Yes, he also got to touch it.

He: What did you think about that?

I: Nothing. I get to see so many.

He: Labia?

I: Yes, and penises.

He: Where?

I: At work.

He: What's your job?

I: I'm a bath attendant.

He: Where?

I: At the Academic Hospital.

He: You bathe the old and sick ones?

I: Yes.

He: Do you like it?

I: Yes, except when there is some old man who has perhaps lived alone and who hasn't washed himself for months… Then the filth can be so ingrown that it's almost impossible to wash it away.

He: Mm.

I: But the most disgusting is when they have long nails with filth underneath.

He: Isn't it strenuous to stand and bathe people all day?

I: Yes, but we have helping devices. Lifts that draw the patients from their beds and lower them into the water, and lifting and sinking bathtubs… We never have to lift heavily or stand bent when we work.

He: Well, that's good.

I: There is some sort of hydraulic device that makes it possible to change the height.

He: I see.

I: And so we bathe them and wash their hair and clip their nails and…

He: …

I: She had almost no hair.

He: Who? Your friend?

I: Yes, my husband would have liked that.

He: You're married?

I: Yes. He usually says that I should shave mine off. "Shave off your cunt hair," he says.

He: …

I: Oh my God! What kind of shit is that? Why does he want me to do that? That's lousy! Why does he want me to look like a little girl?

He: He's maybe a paedophile?

I: Yes, he must be! He wants to fuck children! That's why he doesn't want me to have any hair. Why have I never thought of that before? It's disgusting!

He: …

I: He goes after little boys too.

He: He does?

I: Yes.

…

He: What does he say about you being out like this, then?

I: I don't know. It's none of his business.

…

He: Are you sad?

I: Yes, it feels so lousy that he wants me to be something that I'm not.

He: Don't think about it anymore.

I: No… In any case, we're getting divorced.

He: Is that so?

I: Yes. How about you, are you married or divorced or something?

He: No, I've never been married.

I: But this isn't a good way to meet someone, is it?

He: What do you mean?

I: To bring someone home from the street?

He: No, perhaps not…

I: Then why did you do it?

He: I don't know. To get some company, I suppose.

I: Yes, I just walked there and asked for it. One of these days I'm going to get into trouble, my best friend says.

He: …

I: But it isn't better at home, either.

He: What do you mean by that?

I: That he just fights.

He: Your husband?

I: Yes.

He: Does he beat you?

I: No, he doesn't dare. He doesn't want to risk being reported to the police. But everything else…

He: And so, you take off to town to get away from him?

I: Yes, to get away from all the fighting. But that isn't the only reason I go out.

He: What's more?

I: I can't explain it.

He: No, let's hug instead.

I: Are you the one who plays the piano here?

He: No, it just stands here. Can you play?

I: No.

He: Come here and sit a little closer to me and let me hold you.

I: No, it isn't natural for me to be physically intimate with a person I don't know. I already knew that when I was fifteen years old. When my friend and I began to go out and meet guys, I assumed that you would get to know each other before beginning to kiss and hug. You must know that you like the person concerned, before you begin to express it, I think. But if we didn't let the guys make out a little the first evening, they thought that we didn't like them and didn't want to meet us again. So we had to abandon that principle. But now I'm going to bring it back again, I think.

He: Why did you come with me then?

I: Because I hadn't thought about this yet and because I was drunk.

He: …

I: It's in this situation there is a risk that I could get into trouble.

He: Yes, but you're certainly free to go whenever you like.

I: Not everyone would react like that in this situation.

He: No, but that's how *I* react.

…

I: Oh, why must he be so lousy? Why can't he accept that I don't want to and let me be?

He: …

I: I must give up hope that he will begin to behave normally.

He: Mm.

I: The normal thing is to respect others and not try to force yourself on them.

He: Yes, of course.

I: But he forces himself on those who are small and weak and doesn't care about their protests. To oppress and use others is the only thing he is interested in!

He: …

I: Oh, now I understand! It's *he* who is the devil! Because he's the one who works against me all the time. *He's* the one who cannot stand love and who tries to stop the truth from coming out. It's he! There is no devil! No God either. The only things that exist are truth and lies, and if you want to be free you must choose the truth.

He: Yes, that's for sure.

I: That's why he hates me. He hates me because I won't continue to live a lie. Oh, it's so lousy! If he's sad because I want a divorce, he can just cry! That's what papa did when I was moving from home. I thought he was ridiculous who wasn't happy for my sake, but he didn't try to stop me, anyway.

He: …

I: The things they are sad about don't have anything to do with me. If they could feel where their sorrow belongs, they wouldn't have to take it out on me. Then they would understand that what I do, is all for the best.

Lasse rang and proposed that we should meet again. Eva-Lena wasn't at home, and he felt a little down and said that he missed me. He also thought that we should try to sort out what happened last time we met. And I'm not unreasonable, so I said that he was welcome. Though there wasn't very much sorting out.

He thinks that I am influenced by Eva-Lena and claims that a lot of what I say and believe in comes from her, and if it weren't for that, there wouldn't be any problems between him and me.

But I can't agree with that. What I think and feel and say doesn't have anything to do with her. When I tried to convince him of that, he got angry and threw me down on the bed. Then I decided not to say no, and not to give resistance. I should let him *discover that what happened between us was wrong. Last time I showed that I thought so, but this time* he *was supposed to realize it.*

He had pulled down my pants and carried on with his tongue between my legs, while I tried to overlook that I didn't want it at all and just disappeared into myself. I lay there and watched him, and perhaps I thought: Feel that this is wrong! I had decided that I should be love, and I felt like love, but before he had perceived what I sent out, he only acted according to his own needs. Then he looked up and into my eyes, and that made him unable to continue. Then there was a complete stop! He was forced to disappear.

And that was probably the end. Because then he called from home and said something about his being to little for me and not measuring up. Some other place and some other time it could possibly be something, he said, but not now. He admitted his inability then, I thought, and the situation between us was made clear and stands out in a completely different way than previously. Now I can finally see what divides us, and I couldn't really do that before.

I don't know what it is that drives me to continue writing to Johan, though I sometimes think it's wrong. It's perhaps true, as he says, that he doesn't want my letters. But if it were true, I think I would be able to feel and accept it. Kicki thinks that my involvement with him is damaging and thinks that I should try to get myself out of it. She has read in a book that you can become ill by opening yourself and placing yourself close to a person who holds his feelings inside and who hasn't confirmed himself.

And I know it's dangerous. But how could I abandon him and leave him alone? If I can't do it, it's because I can't be alone myself, Kicki says. If you choose a person who doesn't want you, you're at the same time deselecting yourself.

And I know all that, but I can't help that I love him more than I love myself. How could I stop doing that? Kicki says that I should increase distance from him inside myself and try not to get near him in reality. But since I don't have any boundary to him, how would that work? What would I build that wall of? Contempt and hate? Shall I disdain him because he is weak and unhappy, and hate him because he doesn't love me? But then I must stop understanding and stop loving him and start thinking only about myself. And after hate comes indifference and then you are free… Must it end that way? Yes, if I don't want to throw my life away on something that is hopeless, Kicki says.

But I can't stop loving him. I can give up hope that he will start loving me back, and I can give up my belief in his ability, but I can't stop caring about him and wishing that he some day will be able to set himself free.

So faith, hope, love abide, these three; but the greatest of these is love. (1 Corinthians 13:13)

There are many at work who are half afraid of Kalle, one of our patients, because of his behaviour. He can get very excited and blurt out with anything for no reason at all. But I think I understand him, and I don't have any problems with him. I say what I think to him, just like he does to everyone, and I know that he likes me, because that he has told me himself.

But he is hopeless with his money. Once he was robbed of 50,000 kronor, and I became mad at him and asked him how he could be so senselessly dumb and keep so much money in his locker. I hadn't had any idea of it before, although I'm the one who helps him with his economics. He has a cash box which we have decided that he shall lock in the cabinet, but he sees almost nothing, so I help him keep track of the money and write up how much he takes out when he shops.

But one day when I got into his room, he sat there with the cash box out and carried on with the money in front of a couple of substitutes. I became very upset and scolded him, because that is how I think it happened when he lost that 50,000, that it was some of the personnel who tricked him out of them.

But I was too hard on him, I felt afterwards, so I took it back and apologized. What it was about for my part, I don't really know, but in my anger I felt very offended. I have put in a lot of time and interest in helping him, and then he just destroys it like that! Both he himself and his daughters are very glad that I help him, and then he behaves like it isn't worth a thing! It was me he neglected then, I thought. But it's his money, and if he loses a few thousand more, he can only blame himself. It isn't my problem. That I felt the way I did, I think was because I was reminded of all other times when I have tried to help people without getting anything back. By that I don't mean money or things, but a confirmation of that there has been some importance in what I have done. But you can't always count on that.

I: Yes, hello?
  Johan: Hi, it's me, Johan.
  I: Hello.
  He: You sound breathless?
  I: Yes, I jumped up so abruptly from bed when the telephone rang.
  He: But otherwise things are well?
  I: Yes.
  He: Are you alone?
  I: Yes, Lasse isn't home.
  He: …
  I: How are you, then?
  He: Not very well.
  I: No?
  He: No, I have had a nervous breakdown.
  I: Ah. What were the symptoms of that, then?
  He: I scolded people and was generally unpleasant.
  I: How did it make you feel?
  He: It was like sinking down in a dark hole…
  I: But you feel better now?

He: Yes, I have been to a doctor and gotten medications prescribed so that I'll be able to function normally among people.

I: What kind of medications?

He: Sobril and sleeping pills.

I: But it's no big deal if you don't function among people for a while? Because if you eat tablets you're not able to find out what's the matter.

He: No, but my girlfriend couldn't stand me when I was so labile and nervous.

I: Girlfriend? Someone who lives with you, that is?

He: Lived. She has moved now.

I: Why?

He: Because it was best that way. I couldn't think when she was here. But we had it fucking fantastic in bed!

I: …

He: Hey!

I: Yes?

He: …

I: What are you drinking?

He: Gin and tonic.

I: …

He: I can talk with you about everything…

I: You can?

He: Yes, and I don't mind you continue writing.

I: You don't?

He: No, I think your letters are entertaining and interesting.

I: You do?

He: Yes, but I can only handle a little bit at a time… That letter with forty pages that I got once took a long time to get through.

I: But I don't always write long letters.

He: No, not long, but many, and they come often! One week I got six of them.

I: You couldn't get six in a week?

He: Well, one day two letters came at the same time.

…

I: How did you react in the beginning, when I started to write to you?

He: At first I was flattered and then indifferent.

I: Why?

He: I didn't understand the letters and thought they were unpleasant.

I: Have you thrown away all you have received?

He: No, I don't throw anything away that might be valuable.

I: …

He: I've got rid of all the postcards and cardboard pieces, but I still have the letters. And I have read every one of them.

I: You have?

He: Yes, except for some single ones, that I tore apart in pure anger.

I: Yes, like the one I brought to you myself, when you got so...

He: …

I: Why did you get so angry at that time?

He: I wanted to be left alone. And it was so fucking tiresome to get your letters. Though sometimes, when there has been a temporary break, I have missed them in some way…

I: Why do you think they are tiresome?

He: I don't know. But all I get to know about how you're out in town and…

I: You can take it as something you read in a book or see in a film.

He: Yes, but it isn't.

I: No…

He: …

I: How many cards and letters have you received all together, do you think?

He: I don't know.

I: But an estimate?

He: Seventy-five, possibly.

I: Oh, dear.

He: Yes, it's quite a fortune.

I: …

He: Can you wait a second while I go and fill my glass?

I: …

He: Are you still there?

I: Yes.

He: …

I: Why are you drinking?

He: Because it tastes good.

I: Yes, but why do you always have to drink when you call?

He: It's just the way it is.

I: But why?

He: It's just the way it *is!*

I: But I don't understand.

He: That I drink is uninteresting, I think.

I: Well, I accept facts.

He: No, you don't.

I: I accept that you're unable. But "unable" isn't fun.

He: No, I don't think so, either.

I: You don't want to, then?

He: It isn't a question of *will!*

I: But can't you try to see it from my point of view also? Why should I just sit here and…

He: *As* I have seen it from your side! But what difference does it make that I have been drinking? What does it matter? I'm still reasonable.

I: Yes, but I believe you can do better than that.

He: Ah, you're so delicious! So… *evasive.*

I: …

He: But it's up to you if you want to talk with me or not. Just let me know.

I: You want me to go along with your conditions, but I think that both should be accommodating and not just one of us.

He: Accommodating? Well, that I call you now is accommodating, isn't it?

I: Yes, If I *want* you to call, that is.

...

He: I feel sorry for you.

I: Why?

He: Well, what are you *doing*, then?

I: There is no way you can know what I'm doing.

He: There isn't?

I: No, I don't know what picture you have of my life.

He: Of course I have a picture.

I: Yes, but I don't understand how it looks.

...

He: You don't feel any trust. I do. I'm trusting. I believe that others only wish me well.

I: Everyone except me, that is? I'm the exception who only wishes you pain?

He: No, I know that you don't want that... That I call you now, is actually because I want to ask you if you would like to go out with me and eat on Saturday?

I: Why?

He: Why? Because I like you. You aren't stupid, and I like being together with interesting people. And I have so much I would like to talk with you about...

I: But before you said that you were afraid of me? You aren't anymore, that is?

He: No, I want to meet you.

I: Yes, but must we go out?

He: No, if you don't want to I won't...

I: I don't mind *meeting* you, but I don't want to go out and eat.

He: Ah, everything just splits to me!

I: …

He: Hello?

I: Yes? I'm not saying no to *you*, just to going out.

He: What's your proposal then?

I: I don't know.

He: But now *I'm* the one who wants contact, and then…

I: It's only going to a restaurant I don't want.

He: Why not? Would you feel unsure there?

I: No, but uncomfortable, perhaps.

He: If we eat at my place, then?

I: Yes, that would feel better.

He: Well, let's say so, because I must eat! I'll call you on Saturday about seven.

I: But I find it so hard to believe that this isn't just a whim on your part.

He: No, this has been thoroughly thought through! That I'm calling *just now* is possibly a whim, but I have thought about it a long time.

I: …

He: To just sit and talk… would you get anything out of that?

I: Yes, of course.

He: Nothing sexual?

I: No, nothing sexual.

He: Well, you don't have to *laugh*!

I: No, I'm sorry.

He: I'm not offering you marriage and children or… I can't take responsibility for a child. I have enough of taking responsibility for myself. I won't have children before I'm able to take care of myself.

I: No, you're still so young.

He: It will probably take seven years.

I: Yes.

He: It will take fifteen years.

I: Yes.

He: Twenty-five!

I: …

He: I'll call you on Saturday then.

I: Yes, if you haven't changed your mind before then.

He: No, I won't change my mind.

I: …

He: Bye, then.

I: Bye-bye.

Sobril Anxiolytikum with tension relieving, anxiety dampening and muscle relaxing characteristics.

Indications: Stress symptoms, psychosomatic reactions and neurologic symptoms presentation with fear, unease, muscle tensions, insomnia difficulties, headaches and irritability. Sobril can be experimentally applied to dampen acute anxiety symptoms with treatment of alcohol abuse. Sobril is not advised for psychosis. (Fass)

Johan called and said that he wanted to see me. I will go to his home on Saturday and eat with him. But I don't think it will turn out well. If I am myself when I am there, he will not be able to talk with me, or also I won't be interested in what he has to say.

I don't want to eat with him, either. Why do we have to eat? And he will drink. He said that he isn't afraid of me anymore, but he will drink anyway, and what is the purpose of me going there in that case? Just to sit there and listen to his drunk talk? But I think I've done enough of that on the telephone.

And I don't want to meet him when he smokes. But I can't tell him in his own home that he should go out on the balcony to smoke, so either I must go out there myself every time he lights a cigarette, or also there is no point in going to him at all. It isn't I who should go to him, but he who should come to me, I think, and not just in an outer sense.

I don't understand what he is out for. Does he want someone to lay, or someone to tell his life history to, or someone to help him to change his life? But I don't want to serve that way. I don't mind meeting him, but I don't want to get tricked, so I make a mistake when I'm there. I'm not considering staying over night if he wants me to do that.

I think it's wrong to go there. I don't know what I have there to do. I'm going just because I'm curious. I love him, but he will never be able to accept my love, so there is no reason for me to meet him. We aren't at the same place. I don't want what he can offer, and he can't offer what I want, and I don't know how that will be possible to change.

We didn't meet. He didn't call until late in the evening, when I had gone to bed.

"Hello, hello," he said when I answered.

There was a problem with the phone connection, he claimed.

"Stop playing around and get to the point," I said. "What do you want?"

"I want to apologize for not calling. I got an offer for an airplane flight to Gotland that I couldn't decline, and I got no opportunity to call you and tell you about it. But now I'm apologizing."

"There's no point!" I said.

"No, it's up to you…"

"Yes, and it's just as well that it came to nothing, because you're not interested in my life, and I don't give a shit about yours, so what's the point in meeting?"

"No, if that's how you look at it…"

"Yes, isn't it true?" I said.

And then I hung up on him and unplugged the telephone. I don't understand why he must act like this. If he had changed his mind, he could just have called and said so. I don't understand why he must always shirk and lie.

Many a man proclaims his own loyalty, but a faithful man who can find? (Proverbs 20:6)

On the thirteenth of December it will be exactly ten years since Bosse and I got engaged. It wasn't especially popular at home that we did, I recall. Mamma thought we hadn't known each other long enough, and that I was too young and so on. At the same time, she was glad, because she fancied Bosse.

After that it wasn't long before we moved in together. We moved into my grandma's apartment, which stood empty because she had wound up in eldercare.

And one evening Bosse came home and seemed so distressed. I asked him what was going on, because he looked so serious and seemed so burdened. But he didn't want to admit that there was something wrong. Then I got a sudden thought that said: He can't have children! He is sterile! That hit me directly. But I didn't take it especially seriously, and I thought immediately – I obviously have solutions for everything! – that in that case we can adopt instead. But I felt sorry for him who had to tell me. I tried to help him to get started, and finally he came out with, that he already had children! He said that he had a little girl who lived with his parents.

And then I became extremely disappointed. Not because he had a daughter, but because he hadn't told me. "How could you do like that?" I said. "Well, I thought you wouldn't want to be together with me if you found out." "But how could you believe that I would break up for such a thing?" That was what hit me the hardest — that he could believe something like that about me.

Then I thought that it must have been because he was afraid, that he had been in such a hurry with the engagement. Because he wasn't usually the one who was in a rush. And his sister had said to him: "You haven't told Kicki about it? Certainly, you must tell her about it!" She was mad at him because he hadn't told me that he had a daughter before we got engaged. But every time he was about to say it, he lost courage.

Then he told me about the girl's mother, who he had been together with when he was nineteen years old. When he was supposed to do his military service, she was pregnant, and they got engaged. He called her and wrote letters, and everything seemed well until her mother contacted him and told him that her daughter was running around with others. The mother really liked Bosse and thought it wouldn't be right if he didn't get to know about it, so she told him, and then he broke the engagement in spite of her pregnancy.

His girlfriend was a bit blabbing, I was about to say, but I mean promiscuous, and she drank a lot also, so his parents took care of the girl from the very beginning. Bosse went there regularly and visited her until he met me. Then there was a complete stop, because I didn't know about her, and he and I met almost every evening.

He was forced to resist contact with her only because he hadn't told me the truth. But as soon as I had got to know about it, I said that he must start seeing her again. If he wanted to, I could accompany him sometimes, I said.

In the middle of the night I awoke because I thought the telephone rang. I don't know how many times I have been halfway up from bed before I have realized that the signals were only my imagination or a dream. Then I must lie there and wait for my heartbeat to calm down, before I can fall asleep again.

I don't want to be ready to rush up in the middle of the night to answer the phone. I don't *want* any nightly conversations over the telephone! I want him to call me during the day and when he is sober. But he only dares to call when he is drunk, and it isn't right to let him do that.

It is Johan's inability to separate from his papa, that makes me still stay with Lasse. I can't move away until he is ready for it. But I don't cook for Lasse any longer, and I don't do his laundry, and I don't wash his dishes. He has to buy and prepare his food himself now, and when he wants to wash his clothes he must do it himself by hand, because I don't loan him my washing machine anymore. And I have divided up the groceries and put his things in another cupboard, and in the refrigerator, he has his victuals on a special shelf, so that nothing will get mixed up. I don't sleep in the same room as he any longer, either.

I don't prepare his food, don't wash his clothes, don't wash his dishes, and don't clean his room. He has got pissed about everything I have stopped doing, but I don't care, because I don't want anything more to do with him! Sometimes I can barely stand seeing him. One day when we were quarrelling, I got so mad that I gave him a fist punch on the jaw. Then he fell backwards down in an easy chair and didn't dare get up again. I don't want it to be fights, but that's what happens when he tries to force himself on me.

And sometimes we drink. I don't know why I continue to drink with him when I know how it usually always ends, but every time I hope that I will manage to handle it better than the time before, and eventually he may not be able to force himself on me at all, I think. But I don't drink his whiskey, only my own booze, because otherwise it feels like he gets an advantage.

Here you will see sparks, said the smith, knocked out the tailor's eye. (Saying)

Mamma called and talked about her friend's youngest daughter, who is expecting a baby. Mamma thinks she is too young – she is eighteen years old – and she is worried about how it will turn out for her.

But she wasn't much older herself when she had Anita. She has told me that she was nervous when she was going to tell her mother that she was expecting, because it was before papa and she had gotten married, but afterwards she was only happy. But she was sick while pregnant, and Anita was born prematurely.

And later it became so worrisome, because when Anita got older she escaped from home and shoplifted and took money from both mamma and grandmother. Mamma couldn't manage her and thought that she was so difficult. If she had done something wrong, mamma said to her: "Just wait until papa comes home!" And to papa, when he turned up: "Now you need to deal with Anita, because today she did such and such."

And than papa gave her a beating.

I: What are we going to do here?
  Unknown man: Have a little fun.
  I: But weren't you supposed to give me a lift home?
  He: Yes, I'm going to do that.
  I: What are we doing here, then?
  He: I thought you could help me a little.
  I: With what?
  He: Well, it's been a long time since…
  I: …
  He: What do you say about that?
  I: If you mean that you want to fuck, the answer is

no! I don't lay old men!

He: But I'm not that old, am I?

I: Yes, you're old enough to be my pop!

He: Okay, okay… But may I touch you a little while I do it myself, then?

I: Touch?

He: Yes, fondle.

I: Why?

He: Because it would be pleasurable.

…

I: What are you doing?

He: Open up a bit.

I: …

He: Maybe you'd like to take it in your mouth?

I: No, I won't!

He: No? But let me touch you a little, then.

I: …

He: Oh, what soft and fine tits you have…

I: Watch my bra.

He: Yes, it's just as well that I unfasten it so it doesn't go to pieces.

I: …

He: Yeah, yeah, now it's going a lot better, now I feel your soft, wonderful tits, now I just need to… yes, yes!

I: …

He: Like velvet against my lips…like velvet!

I: …

He: Oh, little girl!

I: Let go!

He: No, let me feel, let me touch you a little, I promise I'll be careful!

I: ...

He: Just spread your legs a little, so that I can reach.

I: ...

He: You're so beautiful, so soft and warm and beautiful!

I: ...

He: Oh, little girl! Let me come in, I promise to be careful, I just want to feel, feel and touch you, so that you get wet, so that you swell and get wet.

I: No, now it's enough.

He: No, let me feel, let me feel that you want to, that you are open and want to, just let me feel your wet, lovely pussy!

I: It isn't wet.

He: Oh, yes, yes, come now, yes, yes, come now, yes, yes... *come*!

I: ...

He: Oh, little girl...

I: Are you satisfied now?

He: Yes, how can I thank you?

I: By giving me a lift home.

He: Yes, I'll do that, of course I'll do that.

I: ...

He: You have no idea how thankful I am for this.

I: ...

...

He: Maybe we could meet again?

I: No, we can't!

He: No, what should a young, beautiful girl like you be doing with an ugly, old dude like me?

I: Nothing!

He: No, quite so, quite so… But you have no idea how much this means to me!

I: …

He: Are you freezing?

I: Yes.

He: It will soon be warmer.

I: No, it will never be warm.

He: Excuse me?

I: It will never be warm, I said!

He: …

I: But I'm not going to stay and freeze to death.

He: No, no…

…

I: You're as stupid as my pop!

He: …

I: I wonder if he also wanted to "feel" me? That's perhaps why he never touched me? Perhaps he didn't dare, in case he would get horny?

He: …

I: And then I married someone of the same kind… Because that's what you do, as long as you are emotionally bound to your parents.

He: …

I: But I don't want to be that way anymore. That's why I do things like this, to be reminded of how it was when I was a little girl and perhaps be sad because I didn't get what I needed. I haven't realized it before, but that's the way it is. Everything you do, has a deeper meaning also, and you must feel it and interpret it and take responsibility for it, if you want to be free.

Sven called. I haven't heard from him for years, so I was a little surprised, but it turned out that he had seen me in town and felt that he wanted to get in touch. After a while he asked if he could come over, but I noticed that he had been drinking, so I said that I don't participate in such things anymore. Sitting and listening to drunk people, I meant, like I have done with him, and like I have done with papa so many times.

I met Sven on a course, and at that time he had a girl, so when he began to show interest in me, I was completely determined that we should meet only on a friendly level. I would just help him with his drinking problem, which I had a feeling that his girlfriend couldn't do. When he felt bad I let him come home to me and had big ideas that he could stay with me and not need to go to a hospital. He could lie on my sofa or bed, and I could keep him company and be by his side when anxiety hit him after drunkenness and help him to detoxify. Oh, yes!

But there were sexual tensions between us also, though I didn't want that. It wasn't the way it had been with Leif, that we needed to get past it so that we could talk, and there wasn't the enormous physical attraction it had been with Peter, that I didn't listen to my head and let my body decide, and it wasn't the way it had been with Åke, that he needed help to manage it. No, in Sven's case it was rather a feel-sorry-for-him-feeling that made me go along with a brief physical intercourse with him also.

To get the opportunity to practise those relief operations, I had to pay, and it was because I had my own sub-conscious interest in it – to help papa, *I realize now. But hopefully, I don't have that need anymore, and that's probably why I could say no to Sven's request now. Sitting and listening to drunk talk I don't do anymore, I felt very distinctly, and that hasn't been quite clear to me before.*

Unknown guy: Why are you standing here, freezing? Are you waiting for someone?

I: No. I couldn't come in.

He: Where?

I: To my friend.

He: Does she live here?

I: Yes, but she didn't let me in.

He: Why not?

I: She doesn't like that I drink. She never has. That's why she didn't let me in.

He: Because you have been drinking?

I: Yes.

He: What are you going to do now, then?

I: I don't know. Find another place where I can drink.

He: Do you have booze with you?

I: Yes, do you want some?

He: No thanks. But you can't stand outside in the cold and drink.

I: Yes, I can.

He: Come home with me instead.

I: Where do you live, then?

He: Just a few entryways away from here.

I: Then you perhaps know my friend?

He: No, I don't think so. I haven't lived here very long.

I: She's rather short and dark haired, and she usually wears a brown, suede fur.

He: No, I don't think I have seen her… Shall we go, then?

I: I shouldn't go with you.

He: We can just sit and talk.

I: Yes, but I don't know you.

He: No, but I don't bite.

I: …

He: Here it is. Watch out for the steps.

I: Yes.

He: How do you feel?

I: I'm fine.

He: Please come in, then.

I: Thanks.

He: You can hang up your things over there.

I: Yes. Oh, dear…
He: Did it go well?
I: Yes. Do you live here alone?
He: Yes. Do you want something?
I: I don't know.
He: Please sit down.
I: Thanks.
He: …
I: I don't want to be here.
He: What did you say?
I: I don't want to be here.
He: You don't?
I: No, not here and not there.
He: Do you regret coming along?
I: No, I don't regret anything.
He: …
I: I can't stand it anymore.
He: What did you say?
I: I can't stand it anymore. I want to die.
He: You want to die?
I: Yes, I can't stand it anymore.
He: What is it, that isn't well, then?
I: I want to die, I want to die, I want to die!
He: Take it easy now…
…
I: She doesn't want me.
He: Who? Your friend?
I: No, my mother.
He: Your mother?

I: Yes, she doesn't want me, and if she doesn't want me I can't cope with living. In that case you can't.

He: Yes, I think you can.

I: No, I want to die.

He: …

I: Kill me then!

He: No, you surely understand that I can't do that.

I: Yes, please kill me!

He: …

I: (start to sing) "Like a bridge over troubled water I will lay me down…" (stop singing)

…

He: Sit up now.

I: …

He: Hey, you?

I: …

He: How do you feel?

I: I don't know. I'm not screaming anymore. I'm almost dead.

He: Isn't it uncomfortable to lie there on the floor?

I: I don't know.

He: Come on, I'll help you up. You can lie down on the sofa instead, if you're tired.

I: (start to sing) "When pain is all around I'll take your part… (stop singing)

He: Come on, now.

I: This has happened to me before.

He: What?

I: It was at home with a Greek guy, whom I didn't

know, either. But I felt that he didn't want to be there.

He: Where?

I: In his student room. Or in Sweden, perhaps. I don't know.

He: …

I: But it's nothing to be concerned about. It's just I who can't resist. Though he isn't helped by my being as little and helpless as he.

He: Who?

I: It's he who should raise himself to my level instead. But he can't, and I have difficulty leaving him. That's why it gets this way sometimes, when I meet someone who strengthens him within me.

He: Now I'm not really following…

I: Where is my purse?

He: …

I: There it is.

He: …

I: Do you want some?

He: No, I'm not in favour of booze.

I: I'm not, either.

He: Even so, you walk around with a bottle of vodka in your purse?

I: Yes. By the way, do you know why the Norwegians have stopped putting ice in their grogs?

He: No?

I: Because he who knew the recipe for ice has died.

He: Yes, that one was good.

I: Are you sure you don't want a dram?

He: Yes.

I: Would you like a cigarette, then?

He: No, I don't smoke.

I: But you have an ashtray.

He: Yes.

…

I: Who are on the photo there?

He: They are my children.

I: Are you married?

He: No, divorced.

I: What are their names?

He: Magnus and Pernilla. Do you have children?

I: No, I can't have them. There is something with my fallopian tubes that doesn't work.

He: That's too bad.

I: Yes… Why did you get divorced?

He: Because of long and lasting disunion, as it's usually called.

I: Was it easy?

He: To divorce? No. But it was the only way out.

I: Yes, it is…

He: …

I: Now I'm drunk.

He: Don't drink any more then.

I: Yes, I will. Do you know the Finnish booze game?

He: No.

I: You should be three persons in a room, and everyone should have a big bottle of booze to drink, and when all booze is gone, one person is supposed to go out, and then the two who remain in the room are supposed to guess who went out. Funny, isn't it?

He: Yes. Watch out for your ash there.

I: Sorry.

He: Shall I help you?

I: No, it's not necessary.

He: Here.

…

I: It was fortunate that Kicki didn't let me in.

He: Kicki? Is she your friend?

I: Yes. It was fortunate that she didn't let me come in.

He: Why?

I: Because you're much nicer than she.

He: …

I: Yes, you are…

He: …

I: Oh, now I'm spilling.

He: Yes, set that aside.

I: Yes… Now I must lie down.

He: Yes, do that.

I: No, it doesn't work. The sofa swings.

He: …

I: When I lay on the sofa, they came running and lifted me up and took me to my room.

He: Who?

I: The keepers. The watchmen of the walls. Then one of them stayed with me and sat there and held my hand. Kind, wasn't it?

He: …

I: The first night I slept on the sofa.

He: Why there?

I: Because the girl in the other bed didn't want to share the room with me. "That fucking whore I won't share a room with!" she said. But she had to move to another room later.

He: …

I: I don't know what the meaning of living is.

He: In that you're not alone.

I: That's why you were drawn to me.

He: Was it?

I: Yes, subconsciously you sensed that we had something in common.

He: Do you think so?

I: Yes. "I don't give a shit about my life, said the farmer, fought with the calf."

He: …

I: I don't know what the meaning of this is, either.

He: What do you mean?

I: That I'm here.

He: Well, both you and I get company for a while…

I: Yes, but I never feel lonely.

He: You don't?

I: No, we're always together.

He: You and your friend?

I: No, I and my… Are you sure that you don't want a dram?

Wine is a mocker, strong drink a brawler; and whoever is led astray by it is not wise. (Proverb 20:1)

Eva-Lena came here and rang the door bell. I noticed that she wasn't sober, and I said that I wasn't interested in meeting her when she was intoxicated and didn't let her in. She had a bottle in her purse and had in view to sit here and drink more. But that came to nothing, because I don't allow such things anymore, and that applies to all, I said to her.

Then she left, and I didn't feel a bit guilty that I hadn't let her in. Because now there is going to be an end of me putting myself aside for the sake of others. Or as they sing in an old song that suddenly popped up in my head: "It's all right now, I've learned my lesson well, you can't please everyone, so you've got to please yourself."

Though now I have a little bad conscience anyway, because I completely cold-hearted sent her out in the winter night with the bottle as her only company… But if it really were my company she wanted, she could have come sober.

Merry Christmas and Happy New Year!

Here is a letter again, instead of a Christmas card and Christmas presents.

You think my letters are entertaining and interesting. No, you think they are sick and unpleasant. You can't handle them, and you don't want them. But I may gladly continue to write to you.

Do you want a swig of vodka? I have a little left in my bottle here. But you perhaps don't like vodka? When this bottle is empty, I can drink beer if I want to, because I have two cans in the refrigerator. I have never liked beer, but yesterday when Lasse and I went shopping at Wessels, and I saw the beer cans there, I felt that I would like to have some and bought two of them.

I smoke and drink. When you were at work, you smoked Prince. I have also changed to Prince. No, I haven't. I smoke Yellow Blend. People in a hurry smoke Kent. "Such is life, such is life, so much falseness there is here. The one you lose, another wins, so hang on to the one you are in love with." (An old hit song)

My lips feel numb. It's a good thing that I don't need to talk, because then I would slur. Stiffly I encircle the cigarette with my lips. No, soft and wet. Would you like me to encircle your penis with my lips? But then it got to be my vaginal lips instead of my oral lips.

I want you to come here. If I take off my clothes and lie down and open my legs, you come and slide into me and kiss me and…

No, it's just fantasies. Everything is fantasies. You don't exist. You're just a figment of the imagination that my brain has created for me to project my dreams and feelings on.

It's so wonderful to be drunk. I'm going to drink and drink, and then you'll come and make love to me. If you're not very randy, I can help you a little. "First you take it, then you drag it, said the old hag, skinned the eel." Yes, and then we could have sexual intercourse. "We will manage this, both old and young, if we unit and spit in our fists." (Old madhouse memory)

I want you to be inside me all the time. When Lasse had sex with me, the muscles in my vagina pushed out his penis, but I know that if it were you who laid me, the muscles would draw you deeper inside me.

I become so randy when I think of it. Why can't we meet and have sexual intercourse? It would be so wonderful, and I would be so sad, and when you came, I would press you hard towards me and never let you come out of me again. Why can't you be here? I want that.

I have already pulled up my shirt and taken out my breasts. But just as difficult as it is for you to suck on your penis, it is for me to suck on my breasts. I can only moisten my nipples with saliva that I have put on my fingers.

Oh, I can't stand it! I must take my pants off, too. "I notice that it's dripping, said the old hag, milked the bull." Yes, it does. I must have something inside me. I don't know what to use. The bottle won't do, because it isn't empty yet. I need to go and get something else. Wait here while I look.

I took a breakfast sausage. I have never used a breakfast sausage before. But whatever you get inside you makes you beautiful, as the girl said.

My breasts are still bare. Can you visualize my breasts? And my stomach and my thighs and my opened legs?

Now I'm pressing it in. It becomes wet and slippery and slides easily. "It goes easy, said the boy when he lied." Why can't it be you? I pretend that it's you. I put my legs close together. You're inside me and can't come out. You fill me. I open my legs and draw out the sausage a bit. I press it in again. Would you like to slide in and out of me like this? I press it in as far as possible. I'm going to leave it there while I take a swig of vodka. Oh, soon I won't be able to stand it any more! "Now, I'm coming, said Billengren, got into time with the waltz." No, not yet. I let it slide out. I press it in. Oh, now I must...

Excuse the interruption, but I had to fix it. Now I must go to the toilet. All this drinking becomes my urine, in contrast to *your* drinking, which will be your ruination. Because while you drink alcohol, I drink just water, milk or juice. I don't have a booze bottle here, and no sausage. How could you know what is true? You can't know if I lie or not, when I write. I perhaps make everything up. You will never know. And I will never know how much you have understood and still don't understand.

Lasse's cock curves to the left. Most men have left leaning cocks,

I have noticed. But yours curves to the right because you lay and held it when you were little, so it was drug to the right. No, that's probably not the reason. I wonder if your cock is as big as Lasse's? His is 19 centimetres in erect condition. (We measured it with a measuring tape once.)

But size doesn't matter. Nor does age. When you call me an old hag, I believe you mix me up with your mother. But then you shouldn't sit and whisper in the telephone that you think I have a sexy voice, because that isn't appropriate to say to your old mom.

Ugh, I almost can't get this down. I have probably had too much of the good, as the Good Templar said when he got water in his knee.

Before, Lasse encouraged me to drink, so that he could have a little entertainment in the evenings. He thought it was fun to sit and listen to my drunk talk. No, I don't know. He probably wanted me to be drunk, so that he could more easily get to lay me afterwards. But I didn't want to lay him no matter how drunk I was.

I don't feel well now. I probably can't tolerate booze anymore. It's probably time for me to be a complete abstainer. But I am an absolutist, because I only drink Absolut Vodka. The last time I finished a bottle, I had to lay on the balcony and sleep all night. That was before I wound up at the Norwegian Embassy. You may not know that place, but I was stationed there a while ago.

(The doctor did his rounds at the hospital and stopped by one of the beds and asked:

"How are you doing?"

"I'm Napoleon," said the patient in bed.

"And who have said that?"

"God have said that."

Then a voice was heard from another bed:

"No, I have never said that!")

When it was nice weather outside we got to sit on blankets on the lawn in front of the embassy building and drink coffee or play frisbee with the personnel. Yes, it was a great time in its way! It was before I listened to reason and became sane.

Lasse isn't at home now. I don't know where he is. I don't care about it, either. It was you who made me realize that I don't love him, and that he doesn't love me. I didn't know what love was before I met you. When I didn't want to lay him anymore, he tried it with my best friend instead, to get back his human dignity. When he didn't get to use his cock for anything but to piss with, he lost his dignity (I didn't know that human dignity was located in the cock!), and he didn't think it was enough to take the thing in his own hands and draw the conclusion himself.

How he solves it now, I don't know. I'm not interested. Nothing about him interests me. He is sick, and he has always been, though I haven't understood it before. He is perverted. I thought it was something wrong with *me* when it didn't feel good to lay him, but now I know that it wasn't because of me. My best friend also thought he was strange. She thinks it has something to do with his childhood and his mother. But I don't give a shit about that. I don't care what the cause of his problems is. That he has to find out for himself (but he never will, because he's too dumb).

I just want him to disappear.

Ulla Bolinder is a Swedish author, born in Uppsala but today living in Knivsta, not far from Stockholm. She has been working at advertising agency, restaurant, hospital, archives and publishing house. Her first book was published in 1997. In her novels she often deals with social issues with emphasis on the individual.

http://www.ullabolinder.jimdo.com